Empty Desk

Janet Call

Empty Desk

Copyright © 2018 Janet Call

All rights reserved.

ISBN:10:1718609426
ISBN-13:978-1718609426

Dedication

This book is lovingly dedicated to my daughters Tamara and Stefanie, who have blessed my life in unbelievable ways; to my grandchildren Jenna, Trevor, and Taylynn, who inspire and enrich me every day; and to my son-in-law Gary, who epitomizes kindness and integrity.

The narratives contained here are largely fictional, but they often reflect my real-life experiences as a public school teacher. These stories acknowledge the many hard-working, creative, and often unrecognized individuals who serve our children in the public schools. They showcase the heartwarming, complicated, and inspirational teenagers who hold the future in their very capable hands.

Empty Desk

Chapter 1

Nelly

It was a warm and unusually humid afternoon in early June when the last bell signaled the end of the school year. Horace Greeley High School unleashed its thousand students and hundred or so staff members for the summer, and the majority raced to the exits. Tattered notebooks, ripped-up posters, and even an occasional abandoned backpack from the recently emptied lockers carelessly lined the hallways, and the classroom doors stood open to release the pent-up stress from final exams, semester grades, and a few reluctant goodbyes. It had been a difficult year, filled with more challenges than most, and everyone welcomed the change that summer invariably brings.

It took less than an hour for the parking lots to empty, the buses to take their final runs, and the staff to head to the nearby pub for the annual end-of-the-school-year celebration. Deann Nelson had stayed behind, and she welcomed the silence reverberating strangely down the corridors. She had just one final goal for her very last day as an English teacher at Horace Greeley High School: to retrieve the contents of the secret drawer beneath her desk before leaving as unobtrusively as possible.

She eased her petite frame into the tattered desk chair, tapped her fingers against the wood grain of her desk, adjusted her wire rim glasses, and glanced around her classroom. She brushed the dirt from her blue jeans and adjusted her frayed shirt. She ran her fingers through her short brown hair and heaved a sigh of relief that this chapter of her life was complete. At sixty-one, Deann figured she probably still had enough years left to exorcise demons of her past and perhaps even to explore her rather extensive bucket list.

For more than thirty years, Deann had been the quintessential high school English teacher who loved perfect grammar and modern poetry, properly documented research papers, and correct spelling. She had Shakespeare committed to memory and could recite a line from Hemingway with uncanny precision. She had once dreamed of becoming a famous author, but life, tragedy, and hundreds of students had distracted her.

Far more important to her than the complexities of language and literature, though, were the relationships she had built with many teenagers whose journeys had taken them into Room 203. Despite her red pen and insistence on "correctness," she rarely lost sight of the human element in the many teenagers whose lives intersected with hers. Despite stark changes in society through those decades, her last class still embodied those same immense fears, dreams, worries, and hopes of the first.

The trademark of her career had been storytelling. She taught through stories, often those from classical writers and contemporary songwriters, and sometimes plaintive tales from epic poems or modern dramas. Nothing, though, compared to the real-life narratives of everyday heroes and villains, and every decade had many of each. High school students had stories of their own, and many of them rivaled Shakespeare or Steinbeck in tragedy or triumph. There was something both comforting and frightening about the way these many real and fictional tales intersected in the high school setting, and Deann Nelson wondered aloud, *Who will tell the stories?*

She had spent the last few months mentoring her replacement and those of a handful of other retiring teachers. These newly credentialed teachers, fresh from the university, were adept at analyzing test scores and generating computerized lesson plans. Armed with intelligence and technical expertise, they arrived with not only eagerness but also the same cocky assurance that Deann herself had once exhibited.

Deann smiled, thinking about the orientation program she had devised for the new hires. It started with the usual details about making copies of handouts, logging into the computer system, ordering supplies, and checking out keys. Then she led them on a tour of the computer labs, library, athletic facilities, greenhouse, teacher lounge, counseling offices, and faculty bathroom. Afterwards, she escorted them to a simple wooden bench under a couple of aspen trees on the remote edge of campus. "This," she said, "is where you will go when you need to cry." She said no more but noted how some of the new teachers somberly nodded, while others merely rolled their eyes.

In this new era of high-stakes testing, she feared that they would somehow let statistics define their "teacher" worth. A long career in education had taught her that it was not numbers but human connections that ultimately mattered most. She hoped that some of them would see well beyond an ACT score or a grade point average. She had long contended that high school educators should concentrate on helping students learn how to enjoy a life as well as how to make a living.

Deann resisted the emotion she felt welling up within her, and reluctantly faced the truth. The digital age had started to change the landscape of learning. Scripted lessons, comparative analytics and constant testing subtly started replacing the creativity and spontaneity that had once been the hallmark of a teacher. Oh, there would still be stories; of this she was certain. But the storytellers were disappearing.

She thought for a moment of some of her own tales and wondered what some of her colleagues and bosses would think if they knew how many of them were based on her own experiences. She had always considered it a wise decision to separate her personal and professional life.

Deann had traveled extensively nearly every summer; her foray into military life in her 20's led to a decent command of Arabic and expertise in handwriting analysis. At one point, she considered a career in the Navy; her wanderlust nature was a good match, but constant military regimentation was far too stifling. The possibility of teaching a subject she loved, coupled with unencumbered summers, led her to Colorado and Horace Greeley High School. This was a decision she never regretted, as it enabled her to accept summer assignments as a questioned documents examiner, and those journeys had led her far from a comfortable existence as a high school English teacher.

She had never married, although she had come close a few times. Those would-be husbands defied the stereotype of spouses of teachers. Each had had a wild past, a thirst for adventure, or an egregious ego. A lover of contrasts, Deann acknowledged she needed something or someone in her life that defied convention. She rationalized that those former relationships had helped her to both understand and engage her students, but in all honesty, she simply preferred to live alone. Thus, instead of settling solely into predictability and a suburban existence, Deann used summers to cultivate her rather wild and adventurous side that bore little resemblance to the sometimes-mundane routines of public school.

Deann had always been a voracious reader and writer, and her love affair with words never waned in spite of the sometimes foul, and always irreverent, language of teenagers. In her tenure in a public high school, she had also opened her heart to her students. Many had nuzzled their way into that cavity, and then trampled around, leaving muddy footprints. Others had entered with tiny knives, constantly carving away at her belief that things could always be better. Fortunately, in times of discouragement, there were always those who filled her deflated heart once more with the genuine hope that the future was indeed still glorious.

As she prepared to pack up, she spotted the most recent folder of odds and ends that she had squirreled away with the thought of someday examining them once again. It contained an eclectic batch of memos, half-written poems, notes she had confiscated from students who could not afford iPhones to text, requisition forms for field trips that the district would never fund, and writings that had amused or impressed her. It occurred to Deann that her career had been like that folder, a loosely contrived container bursting with vaguely connected secrets and plans about to spill out into the universe. With just a moment's hesitation, she pitched the folder and its contents into the trash can.

This was the final day Ms. Nelson would erase the white board, turn off the computer, check for new graffiti on the desks, and turn out the lights to room 203. A mountain of old memos and files from classes that had long ago been removed from the curriculum already took up the center of the room. The faint odor of ancient mimeographed copies lingered, and for a fleeting moment, the faces of her very first Honors English class flashed in front of her. All at once the sadness settled in.

The sadness was not because her career was over, and no marching bands had shown up to see her off. It was not sad because her replacement, armed with statistics and mounds of data, had already stripped student poetry and pictures of exotic places from the walls. It was not sad that replacement graphs and charts indicating the school's standardized tests scores had erased the human faces behind those numbers. It was not even sad that the pathetic excuse for a principal had not stopped by to thank her. No, this day was sad because Deann knew that her departure meant that there would be no one left *to tell the stories*.

Chapter 2

Nelly

Deann, affectionately known as Nelly to her students, had deliberately made sure that her final exodus would be alone and unobserved. She knew she needed some time to dismantle the hidden drawer within her desk and remove its contents. The drawer had been expertly crafted by a former student who was failing his Senior English class. Although he could expertly use tools to build just about anything, he could demolish the English language as soon as he opened his mouth. His struggles in English had led to construction of the drawer, and it had served as the reservoir of dozens of secrets Nelly would keep over the years.

Javier had been close to graduating both of his senior years, ultimately only needing a "D" to pass Senior English to walk the graduation line and pick up his diploma. That had been decades ago, and Nelly recalled brokering the deal.

"Build me a secret drawer," she told him, "and memorize and recite a poem. Complete these two tasks and you will never have to open another book. That is, unless some day you want to open your mind to the world of ideas once again."

"Sounds cool to me; it ain't gonna take me long neither," Javier replied.

He delivered on his promise, precisely chiseling a perfectly matched false bottom for the wooden desk and designing a spring latch that was invisible to anyone but Nelly. As he had worked, he sheepishly but proudly rattled off "Dream Deferred," a Langston Hughes poem he had selected because it was so short. He had no idea why anyone would want a secret drawer, but it did not matter if he could manage to get out of the school with a real diploma, something none of his siblings had been able to do.

At the time, Nelly herself did not a have a plan for the drawer; she just wanted to give a kid from a long line of high school dropouts a moment to shine, and she was wise enough to know that his chance of passing Senior English with any of her colleagues was non-existent. He had not earned credit for the course, but maybe a diploma would keep one more poverty-stricken family off the welfare rolls, and perhaps the message of that Harlem Renaissance poet would one day remind him of the possibility of reaching his dreams. Nelly recalled how happy he had been on that graduation day so many years ago when he had run over after the ceremony to hug her, the faint smell of alcohol wafting around him.

Although certain that the building was empty, Nelly rose to make sure that the door to her classroom had been locked, then bent down and felt for the release latch. She could not have known how handy that secret drawer would become, and she was strangely reluctant to open it.

Chapter 3

Jordan

Nelly fingered the gauge that unlocked the secret drawer, pushed it firmly, and jumped when she heard its powerful snap. It was as if the secrets of her career had suddenly been released from captivity. The contents spanned decades, and Nelly affirmed her resolve to guard some of these secrets forever.

The first item Nelly located was the frayed, grimy identification card for David Martin, a pimply-faced, timid looking middle school kid from Newark, Ohio. David Martin had probably been about thirteen at the time the picture had been taken. This was the year David had left that gritty Midwestern town with his well-meaning, but ill-equipped, unemployed mother. This was the year the two of them had fled all connections to his father, a felon bent on revenge. This was the year that the boy left behind his former life and ceased being David Martin. This was the year before Nelly first met the young man she had only known by the name of Jordan Michaels.

In the few years Nelly had become acquainted this boy, she had come to appreciate him as the most remarkable teenager she had ever met. His life was an epic novel by the time he reached adulthood, and if she had never picked up this card from the floor under Jordan Michael's desk many years ago, she would never have learned the intricate plots and powerful themes that permeated his life.

Unwilling to dwell on David Martin a.k.a. Jordan Michaels just yet, Nelly opened the duffel bag that would hold the secret drawer's contents and dropped the card into it.

Chapter 4

Nelly

Nelly grinned, thinking of the fact that no one had ever discovered her little cache of artifacts. To most, the motley assortment of papers and knickknacks would look like a bunch of trash, but to Nelly they represented what had amused, inspired, or transformed her over the course of her career. Most of the items were deeply personal to her, but a few were both dangerous and damning to others, and Nelly had always harbored a vague worry that these secrets might somehow be revealed.

She glanced at the first paper, which had already started to turn a pale shade of yellow. At first, she wondered why she had saved the paper at all. At the top of the page was the standard definition of a simile, a common term in the study and analysis of poetry. She glanced at the words at the top of the page: *A simile is a comparison of two unlike things, using the words "like" or "as."* The examples that followed were standard fare: *Life is like a box of chocolates; you never know what you're going to get. Her eyes were as warm as the sun on a lovely spring day.*

She scanned the document to view the odd collection of original similes that her students had written. Some were spectacular comparisons, others quite predictable, but a few were absolutely hilarious. The bad examples students had written were so outrageously pathetic that she kept them for the sole purpose of producing a good laugh. Over the years, she had resisted the temptation to hold up them up for ridicule, but over time these gems made great models for the *Not-all-similes-work* lesson years after the original authors graduated, or in some cases, dropped out.

She smiled at the first few examples:

Her hair glistened in the rain like urine in the toilet before flushing.

His time was short, like my Uncle Pete.

He was as useful as dryer lint stuck to a pair of boxer shorts.

George Bush's teeth were like tiny white fences, keeping out the weeds.

Suddenly she stopped smiling. There was Martin's simile, an ironic prediction of his fate: *The explosion was terrifying, much like the feeling you get when your dad chases you around with his power saw.*

Ms. Nelson remembered how she had felt the first time she had read those words, at first amused at the ridiculousness of the idea, then later horrified that what he had written had foreshadowed a very real tragedy. Not long after Martin had written the comparison, Nelly learned that his father, Bill Comparo, an inmate at the Centennial Correctional Facility, was serving a three-year sentence for domestic abuse. By the end of that school year, though, Mr. Comparo met the conditions for parole, returning to his Greeley home and family. Ten days later, he fell into a drunken rage and began beating his wife. As Martin tried desperately to protect his mother, his father grabbed a nearby whiskey bottle and violently slammed it into Martin's temple, abruptly ending his son's life.

That was the thing with words. They had innate power; they could always come back to haunt us, or tempt us, or even destroy us. Many times during her career, a hastily written note became the source of months of teenage drama; at others, words transformed and even saved lives. Occasionally, a poem or essay became a heart-wrenching confession or an ironic prediction of a student's fate. More powerful than any other weapons or tools, simple words were proof of what it meant to be a human being, and high school students used them in unbelievable ways.

Nelly set the similes aside and picked up another paper. A young man named Winter Frost had written the next document, a splendid science fiction short story entitled *Shards*. Winter, like the others whose parents thought they were clever in naming their children, had survived his fair share of teasing in school.

Nelly had never produced children of her own, but she knew how important a name could be, and reflected quietly on some of the more memorable ones. What were some of these parents thinking? School could be excruciating at times, but even more so for someone with a weird name. She recalled the most troubling of her career: Dick Hunter, Anita Mann, and Flower Power.

Occasionally there were even sets of twins who shared not only the same gene pool, but also double ridicule because of their parents' decision. Nelly had been impressed with a kindhearted kid named Pinto Bean enrolled in her Mass Media class; she had laughingly commented on the name choice one day in the teachers' workroom. It was then that Mrs. Boring, who had the worst possible teacher name herself, revealed that Pinto's twin sister Lima was taking her Geometry class. Years later, Nelly met Orangejello and Limejello, the Salaad twins.

Empty Desk

As the years passed, the student body became increasingly diverse, and the names harder to pronounce, and the students more difficult to understand. Nelly resisted resorting to the administrators' habit of using "Hey, you" or "Bud," and resolved to pronounce each and every name exactly as the student wished, a policy that opened her up to both criticism and respect.

Nelly fingered a thank-you note that she had almost forgotten about that included a graduation picture of the ever-smiling, good-natured Joseph P-h-u-c-k-e-r. The first time she had spotted the name on the roster, she recoiled, hoping against hope that it was not pronounced the way she thought.

High school teachers are generally immune to profanity, as it often came with the territory. However, the protocol at that time was to address students as Mr. or Miss followed by their last names, and Nelly inwardly shuddered at the possibility of saying that word for an entire semester in front of a group of tenth graders. Nelly decided it must be French, so she carefully pronounced it *Foooo-Care,* but Joseph immediately corrected her, confirming her worst fears.

It was a long semester, and a struggle each time she asked, "What do you think, Mr. Phucker?" She correctly predicted that the mere mention of the word would send the class into a frenzy. When the students had no answers for the questions she posed, they giddily urged her to "Ask Phucker."

Nelly could still see his sheepish expression and the warmth in Joseph's eyes. He was probably the only kid she had ever taught who could handle the consequences of such a label. She heard he wanted to become an astronaut and chuckled at the possibility of Lester Holt or Brian Williams announcing his accomplishments to the world. She wondered what had become of him after graduation.

Chapter 5

Jordan

Not ready to discard the papers just yet, she added them to David Martin's ID already in the duffel bag.

Nelly recalled the very day Jordan Michaels joined her Dramatic Literature class when he first enrolled at Horace Greeley High School a full month after the start of that school year. At the time, she no idea that he was living under an assumed name. She just figured he was probably a product of divorced parents, shuffled to a new school to accommodate some court-imposed squabble over custody.

Nelly had made a special point over the years to help the "newbies" adjust to their new school. Navigating high school was a challenge for the sturdiest of students, and she knew that without a little nudge even the nicest kids often ignored an unfamiliar face. She started the process by encouraging Kevin Jantz and Patrick Gilliland to include Jordan in their break-out group. Eager to please their teacher, they invited him over to the popular table to help them analyze the character Amanda from *The Glass Menagerie*.

Nelly observed the quiet Jordan interact with his classmates. At first, he kept his eyes lowered and his expression unreadable, but before long it was his incisive comments that became the centerpiece for the required oral report to the class. Jordan refused to be the presenter, though, relinquishing his astute observations to the loudmouth Patrick, who enjoyed coming across as a scholar for once.

As the days went on, Jordan retreated to himself, preferring to enter the classroom early, open his text, and write furiously in his notebook. Nelly observed his clothing and backpack for clues about his past and his home life. He thwarted her attempts to get to know him with polite but definite rebuffs. Each day Jordan, dressed in blue jeans and a plain shirt, repeated the pattern of the previous day, and before long, he became virtually invisible, just another nondescript boy getting by in high school.

As time passed, though, Nelly knew intuitively that he was likely hiding something. She noted the way he listened intently to the tales she would tell of Oedipus or Prometheus. She watched the surreptitious habit he had of observing his classmates closely, and instinctively realized he was harboring some kind of secret. Although he only spoke when asked a question, it was as if he really wanted to belong, to lead, but some invisible harness always curtailed him.

His grades were solid, consistently in the A-/B+ range, but Nelly knew he was holding back. When she graded his essays, she would catch the places where he erased a correctly spelled word and replaced it with a mistake. At times, she spotted the places where he had inserted unnecessary commas or made an obvious grammatical error. She was puzzled but allowed the kid his secrets.

Satisfied that he was not likely to be a victim of abuse or one of those undercover detectives passing as a high school student to bust a drug ring, Nelly went about the business of teaching and forgot about Jordan for a while.

One day, though, while she was waiting for the lesson plan fairies to inspire her, she noticed that Jordan had opened his backpack to reveal an intricate panel of zippered pockets and layered flaps. This was no Target backpack, and she watched him as he deftly pushed buttons and tiny clasps to retrieve the items he needed. Realizing she was observing him, Jordan quickly threw his backpack on the floor and resumed his studies.

The class period passed with the usual difficulties of a Monday morning, and the students left in a noisy and rowdy cluster to head to the gym for an assembly. It was then that Nelly noticed the card lying on the floor that had fallen out of Jordan's backpack. She picked it up to see a younger version of Jordan, a picture that captured a middle school boy named David Martin from Newark, Ohio.

What is his story? Why has he changed his name? That day Nelly slipped the card into the secret drawer and headed to the gym. Over the semester, though, Nelly learned that Jordan was simply trying to be as invisible as possible, and he had good reason to do so. If he excelled too much, Jordan reasoned, a teacher would be likely to make a big deal about it. If he wore brand name clothes or Jordan sneakers, not that he could afford them, other students would notice. If he were too loud or sociable, students would include him in their groups. And Jordan wanted no part of any of this.

Chapter 6

Nelly

Nelly had acquired her own nickname from a student from the early 70's who had been one of her favorites. Darren Autoby was every teacher's dream student: smart, funny, sociable, kind, and talented.

In those early days, Ms. Nelson had her own unorthodox punishments to keep her students in check. If students came late to class, their punishment was to sing a song in front of the class. The overwhelming majority of adolescents would rather die, so when the warning bell rang, a virtual thunder of racing footsteps reverberated down the south hallway to room 203. Ms. Nelson rarely had tardy offenders, and the principal at the time tolerated her plan because it saved him dozens of referrals.

One warm spring day, though, when Darren could hardly bear to part with his golden-haired girlfriend Chloe, he entered the room with a saucy look of sheer testosterone a full ten minutes late.

"Ms. Nelson, Ms. Nelson, Darren is really late," declared Addie, the resident suck-up.

"Very well, Darren, you will need to sing a meaningful song to the class. Now. In front of everyone. You will need to enunciate the words and deliver the lyrics with expression. No silliness. Let's have it."

Twenty-seven sets of eyes focused on the charming boy with long shaggy hair and flushed cheeks. Darren gulped,

Empty Desk

smiled, walked over to Ms. Nelson, grabbed her hand, and escorted her to the front of the room, where he indicated she was to take a seat. She complied, looked up, and gazed in shocked astonishment as the guilty offender belted out a flawless rendition of Earth, Wind and Fire's "Reasons" to the delight of his classmates.

Twenty-seven sets of eyes gazed at the now blushing Ms. Nelson, who did the only thing she could think of. "Again," she ordered, "Sing it again." This time Darren glanced around the room, found the averted eyes of the painfully timid, desolate Sarah Goodwin. He sauntered to her desk, and realizing the very real enormity of her embarrassment, he picked up her book rather than her hand and while gazing at it lovingly, he crooned Manhattan's "Shining Star" in tones so velvety that even the jocks in the room were a little starry eyed. When he finished, the now flushed Sarah could only whisper, "Oh, my goodness," the only sound anyone had ever heard her utter. She flashed her first faint smile, and from that moment on, Ms. Nelson loved that tardy boy with the long shaggy hair.

It was such an easy transition to go from the lyrics of those songs into the poetry lesson for the day, and so it was that Ms. Nelson and Darren staged other in-class concerts, unbeknownst to the rest of the class, who simply thought that Darren had probably come to class late because it was spring, and Chloe was a good kisser under the bleachers. From those carefully chosen songs, the stories and discussions of love and betrayal, promise and disappointment, success and failure, ensued.

Darren Autoby accepted Ms. Nelson's quirky teaching, and by doing so, so did the rest of the class. When she placed masking tape on the carpet to teach kids how to diagram sentences, Darren was the first to volunteer a sentence to match the configuration. When she wanted students to analyze how Holden Caulfield might adapt to a new location, it was Darren who helped her put sticky notes on her students' foreheads. He enthusiastically composed the first of many Shrink Lits that lined the bulletin board.

When she insisted that students would be able to understand punctuation better by a neighborhood tour and the class let out a collective groan, Darren declared, "Come on, guys, let's go. It'll be cool."

"See that gate—the hinge—that's just like the semicolon," she would point out.

Ted Drule, always the smart aleck, would make fun of her. "Look, I just stepped on a question mark, Ms. Nelson."

The students would laugh, but Ms. Nelson would take it in stride. Eventually, one of the students would get it. "That stop sign—looks like a period to me."

"The flagpole, the flagpole! It's an exclamation point!"

Ms. Nelson would smile. "Yes, it is. It is used sparingly, but truly stands out to emphasize something important."

"Wow!!"

A few days after the punctuation lesson, Henry Solis sauntered into class with his epiphany on commas.

"I went canoeing with my old man this weekend, Ms. Nelson. I was telling him about that grammar lesson the other day. You know what? The paddle hitting the water over and over—that's kinda like a comma, right?"

"Exactly! It separates items in a series," Ms. Nelson replied.

"You're a genius, dude," Darren piped up. "You get commas. Now tell us about the canoe trip." Then Henry's story began, and the students sat spellbound as Henry relayed his experience rafting down the Colorado River.

Other stories would follow. Often they were just brief expositions, quick anecdotes from weekend trips, or tiny, squeaking denouements, but whatever the details, Ms. Nelson would work them into the fabric of Romanticism or punctuation or research papers. Often it was Darren whose larger-than-life presence would foster the Nelson stories.

"Whooooaaaa, Nelly. Whooooaaaa Nelly," he would cajole, "Tell us a story now. We need a story." His classmates were a little shocked that a student would give the teacher a nickname, but Nelly seemed to fit.

"Yeah, tell a story," the class would chime in. *And she would.*

Chapter 7

Jordan

A few days after Ms. Nelson found David Martin's ID card on the floor, she had an opportunity to talk to Jordan Michaels about it. They were alone in the classroom, and the dismissal bell had already rung. Students had quickly raced to the parking lots or had gathered in noisy herds waiting for the buses.

Jordan sat silently in the first row, glancing furtively from time to time at the empty hallway.

"Is there anything I can help you with, David? I mean Jordan."

The boy's face blanched and for a moment Ms. Nelson thought that he might faint. She jolted from her desk and headed over to where he sat with his copy of *East of Eden* opened to the final chapter. "Are you OK? Can I get you some water?"

Jordan took his time answering his teacher. "I am fine. Why did you call me David?" He looked at her intently, almost fearfully. Ms. Nelson gazed at the young man, noticing that he was wearing the same scuffed shoes, jeans, and blue tee shirt that he had worn almost every day.

"It is just that I found a card on the floor the other day. It had your picture, but the name on it was David Martin. I must have been thinking of that card. Do you want to talk about it?"

Empty Desk

He did not, at least not that day, but over his four high school years Jordan Michaels revealed his story to Ms. Nelson in a series of private after-school conversations. They came in small halting confessions, out of order, jumbled, much like the young man's life. His piercing blue eyes filled to the brim a time or two, and Ms. Nelson could only marvel that David (now Jordan) held fast to his dream of a college degree. She decided early on to guard his secrets, convinced that here was a young man so extraordinary that she would not, could not, ever betray him.

Chapter 8

Nelly

Nelly broke from her reverie, then reached down to retrieve a paper that had been precisely folded into quarters.

I wonder what this is, she thought, as she unfolded it carefully.

For a moment, the unusual Xeroxed photograph of the two enormous butt cheeks puzzled her. It had been many years since she had tucked away that picture as leverage against Zachary Parker.

Zach had been Nelly's student aide decades before. He was one of those out-of-control but likeable teenagers, who would one day grow up to be a good man if he could just learn a little self-control. It was Zach who had painted the genitalia of the massive bighorn sheep statue that guarded the entryway to the school. It was Zach who, with the help of some other derelicts, had raced his motorbike through the hallway of the school to celebrate the end of the CSAP tests. And it was he who had been the ringleader of the legendary water balloon catapults off the school roof and unto the administrators' cars.

The problem with Zach was that he never knew when to stop and he had the uncanny bad luck to always get caught. His harmless pranks turned into petty crimes and a less than stellar behavior record. Zach became Nelly's aide at the request of his frustrated parents and an even more frustrated administration when he pulled off the greatest caper of all: Bra-gate.

Bra-gate was the title given the mission to steal Henrietta Porter's bra and display it on the flagpole to herald the start of spring break. For years, her male students had marveled at the sheer enormity of their Psychology teacher's breasts.

Physics students had wondered about the phenomenon of her being able to stand upright. The girls who had yet to develop any curves consoled themselves with the fact that at least they were not a freak show like Porter.

On one occasion, Zach, totally enamored with the spectacle, had mistakenly said *mammary* instead of *memory* when answering one of Mrs. Porter's questions. Even the male faculty members had shared their awe over a Friday afternoon beer or two.

However, this time Zach had gone too far. To prove his supremacy as the greatest prankster in Horace Greeley High history, he waited until freshmen orientation, a required evening event for all faculty, and a time when Mr. and Mrs. Porter, both teachers, would not be home. He rounded up a few pliable friends, and headed to the home of his well-endowed teacher. The quartet of teenagers took turns chugging a gallon of milk to solidify their mission. Then, wearing camouflage and waving flashlights, they snuck into the back yard of her modest suburban house, giddy with bravado.

"What size do you think she is? I bet she's a 50DDDD."

"No," Zach replied, "She has to be an XXXX. Maybe she has to special order her bras from China or some place."

"Quiet! Let's get in and get out."

To the absolute surprise and relief of the boys, the side door to the garage was unlocked, enabling the four of them to get inside without doing any damage and, more importantly, without detection. In those days, home security systems were non-existent, and houses were often left unlocked.

The four outlaws glanced around at the tastefully decorated living room, scanned the kitchen, and within minutes, they found their way to her bedroom, where they opened a couple dresser drawers, located her lingerie, and grabbed the first bra they could find. The boys gasped in absolute astonishment. "Holy cow!" For a moment, the enormity of the fabric and the sturdiness of the wire under the cups paralyzed them. Phil Kennison held the prize tentatively but triumphantly until Zach seized it, waving it like an Olympic flag. He took a moment to model it for his now cheering buddies. In his excitement, he managed to trip over a pair of shoes on the floor.

"You idiot. Let's get out—now!" yelled his buddy Tyler. "My old man will kill me if we get caught."

"Quit being such a chicken shit," Erik said. "We can outrun any pig in town."

The four glanced around the room, making certain that it looked just the way it had when they entered. Satisfied that nothing was out of place, they left the room and the house as stealthily as they had entered. Not a single one of them noticed that Zach's school ID had fallen out of his pocket when he had tripped over Mrs. Porter's size 9 slippers.

Empty Desk

The quartet headed back to Zach's house where they planned what to do next. After much discussion, they agreed that they needed a banner and a conspicuous place to display their trophy. Zach's parents were home at the time, and he told them that they were working on a project for their psychology class. Mrs. Parker was so pleased that the boys were excited about school work, so she offered to go to Walmart for whatever supplies they needed. When she returned, the boys set to work on their project.

The rest is school legend at its finest. A banner saying **Compliments of Henrietta Porter**, a pink 52G bra the size of Texas, and Old Glory itself waved proudly over the school the next morning.

By afternoon, Zach was in Principal Weaver's office, surrounded by his parents, his probation officer, Mr. and Mrs. Porter, and two Greeley police officers who were trying desperately to stifle their amusement.

This time, though, it was no laughing matter, and Zach knew when he saw his school identification card sitting on the principal's desk, that his penchant for getting out of trouble had expired. After much negotiation, promises and even some tears, the charges for breaking and entering, theft, and trespassing were tabled temporarily. What would happen next would depend on Zach's self-control. That is when Nelly came into the picture.

Mrs. Porter was so humiliated and upset that she rightfully refused Zach admission back into her course. Mr. and Mrs. Parker agreed to pay for tuition so the Psychology course could be completed by correspondence and set about finding a place for Zach to be during that period. Principal Weaver was not about to allow Zach an unsupervised free hour.

After approaching a few of Zach's former teachers to accept him as a student aide and getting no takers, Ms. Nelson felt sorry for the repentant kid and agreed to take him on. For weeks, Zach was dependable and even helpful; however, Deann knew that trouble was a seductive temptress for Zach. She recognized that the slightest transgression would lead to expulsion and time in one of those juvenile detention centers. She reminded Zach of this often.

Unfortunately, Zach's memory was short. One afternoon, after spending a solid thirty minutes at the copier, carefully counting, collating, and stapling, boredom took over. Curious about what his butt would look like if he copied it was too much for him. He unzipped his jeans, pulled down his boxers, hopped up on the Xerox machine, and pressed three. As quickly as he could, he jumped down and readjusted his clothing.

As Zach's luck would have it, the Xerox machine jammed on the second copy. At that instant, he realized that freedom as he had known it could soon be a distant memory. After all, he had used Ms. Nelson's code number, so it would only be a matter of time before he would be busted.

But this was a resourceful kid. He spotted Randy Hollister, a special education student who could often be seen roaming the halls. Unlike Zach, Randy could meander around without a hall pass because he did not bother anyone and he never damaged property.

"Psst. Psst. Randy, come over here."

Empty Desk

Randy heard Zach but was instantly suspicious. The popular students rarely paid attention to the special education kids, and Randy doubted anything good could come out of this. Despite the fact Randy rarely spoke or made eye contact, he could sense the urgency in Zach's tone.

"What?" he mumbled.

"Go get Ms. Nelson in Room 203. Tell her Zach has an emergency in the copy room. Please, please, please." Something about that last *please* reminded Randy of the desperation he sometimes heard in his mother's voice when she could not get through to him. He said nothing but turned around and headed toward Ms. Nelson's room. For three and a half agonizing minutes, Zach had no idea if his message had been delivered.

As soon as Ms. Nelson heard the word *emergency*, she had a suspicion that Zach might have crossed the line yet again. She hurried down to the copy room and within a few seconds realized Zach's dilemma. She quickly opened the machine, deftly lifted out the offending butt shots, turned the pages over, cleared the copy order, and ordered Zach to follow her.

On the way back to the classroom, they crossed paths with the principal. "Problems, Ms. Nelson?" inquired Mr. Weaver as they headed back to Room 203.

"Not a one," Ms. Nelson countered.

When they got back to the classroom, Ms. Nelson tore up the first of the photos into tiny pieces but folded the second and set it aside.

Zach started in with the apologies and promises, but Nelly held up her hand.

"Do you realize that you could be charged with indecent exposure and have to register as a sex offender for the rest of your life? Are you out of your mind?"

Ms. Nelson's disappointment in Zach was evident and he started to cry. As the wet, sloppy tears coursed down his cheeks, Nelly recalled a time in her own life when she had made a stupid mistake, and her commanding officer had saved her. She remembered a forgery case she had worked on that past summer, one resulting in a significant jail sentence for a young mother who naively followed her boyfriend's instructions. All people make mistakes, but Zach Parker had already gotten far too many second chances. Ms. Nelson considered the possible consequences, ultimately deciding to rein in his impulsiveness by requiring him to think of others.

"Zach," she declared, "I could call your parents, the principal, even the police. But I don't think they could help you. You have had it too easy, and you just do not think things through enough. Therefore, I am going to give you one last non-negotiable opportunity to grow up. You will do what I tell you in the way I tell you to do it, or I will expose you for the ass you are. Pun intended. I have the proof right here, and I am keeping it. If you screw up, this photo and your thoughtless actions get passed on to the authorities." Zach looked at her through tears, extended his right hand to shake hers, and gave his solemn vow. "Anything you say. You have my word."

Ms. Nelson then outlined Zach's next challenge: to befriend the lonely Randy, who had rescued him from a more serious consequence than he could have ever imagined. For a long time now, Ms. Nelson had wondered about that lost soul who sauntered the halls; she had never seen him interact with another human being, but she had observed his artwork in one of the study halls she had supervised. She knew that he needed much more than a teacher or a course could provide; he needed a friend, and Zach would become that friend. Ms. Nelson knew that just telling Zach to be Randy's friend would never work. He needed some prep work first.

The following week Ms. Nelson required Zach to research Asperger's Syndrome and to discuss with her what he had learned. He talked openly and thoughtfully about the subject, pausing to comment on how hard it would be to adjust to all of the sounds and distractions of high school.

Next, she arranged for Zach to assist her colleague Joan in the adaptive physical education class. There he partnered up with a student who was recovering from a leg amputation due to an accident caused by driving drunk. As Zach's awareness of both inherited and acquired disabilities grew, some of his swagger and silliness dissipated. Zach could not help but wonder where this path would lead and just what Ms. Nelson had in mind.

When she felt Zach was ready, she arranged for Randy to be her second aide. Knowing that Randy was a skilled artist and that Zach could be quite creative himself, she assigned them a project. Their challenge was to devise a 3-dimensional bulletin board capturing the essence of Henry David Thoreau.

"Who's Thoreau?" said Zach.

Empty Desk

Ms. Nelson smiled at Randy. "Are you familiar with Thoreau?"

Randy shook his head, and Ms. Nelson glanced at Zach. "The two of you will just have to figure it out. You have a week and I want something spectacular." She returned to the stack of research papers she had been grading and listened as the two awkwardly began their work.

Their partnership started with them finding some background on the author, and while doing so, both discovered a connection to the author. Randy was drawn to the idea of living simply and alone at Walden's Pond. Zach was more impressed with the writer's penchant for civil disobedience.

Within a few days, they transformed the six square feet of wall space into an incredibly colorful, interesting, and informative display. The project broke the ice, and the two worked well together. It was fun to watch them high-five one another once the finishing touches were complete.

That semester she vicariously experienced the evolution of a truly unique and close friendship that would last for decades. As the unlikely friendship grew, Zach matured into a kind and decent adult; he began to include some of the more isolated students in group projects and lunch trips to Taco Bell. Once quite a jerk himself, he could recognize the trait in others and did his best to call out others for cruel remarks. Randy started to make eye contact and developed more social interactions with others. Their two very different worlds converged often, and Ms. Nelson loved hearing their chatter and laughter echoing down the hallways.

Randy and Zach graduated the same year, and their families co-hosted a graduation party at the golf course clubhouse. On the invitation, Zach had penciled in *I don't know if you can make it, Ms. Nelson, BUTT Randy and I hope you will be there.*

She was.

Chapter 9

Jordan

It was on a particularly grey winter day that Nelly first learned how David came to be called Jordan Michaels. His story began when fifteen-year-old Precious Chamberlin, the product of two strung-out hippie parents, had bedded down with 19-year-old David Martin in the back seat of a blue 1968 Mustang.

By the time Precious turned sixteen, she got her parents' permission to marry David in a dingy chamber of the Newark, Ohio courthouse. Just days before David Jr. was born, her mother died of breast cancer; the loss so devastated her father that he had become unhinged, and even the birth of a healthy grandson did little to change his perspective. As a result, Precious dropped out of school, moved into a dump of an apartment with her new husband, and tried as best she could to take care of her newborn son. Before long she began peddling weed with her young husband to keep their baby in diapers and food.

The baby daddy had good intentions at first, but being just nineteen himself and not knowing his own absentee father, it was not long before he stopped smoking joints at Indian Mound Park and began his gradual descent into the dangerous life of armed robbery, drug running, and eventually meth addiction.

Precious realized early that her son was bright; he talked and walked well before the expected benchmarks. His fascination with taking apart toys and successfully reassembling them was nothing short of remarkable. Thus, despite her own deficiencies as a parent and her disappointment in not graduating herself, she resolved to make sure that her son had a chance for a real future. Unfortunately, David Sr. did not share her sense of responsibility to young David, truly deserving the label of *Sperm Donor* rather than *Dad*.

David Martin's once booming marijuana business developed some stiff competition, and he started spending more time with the other seedy and sometimes violent thugs of the central Ohio drug world. Some nights he did not come home at all; at other times, he appeared at odd hours with men who scared both Precious and young David. It did not take long for the young family to disintegrate. By the time David turned three, Precious already came to the conclusion that if her child were to ever thrive, the two of them would have to leave her husband and perhaps even Ohio.

After one particularly loud shouting match between Precious and David and confirmation of their suspected drug activity, the property owners kicked them out of their Section 8 housing. Reluctant to stay any longer with her husband and concerned for her son's safety, Precious tracked down an old friend, and for a while she and her young son did their share of couch surfing in the rundown apartments of other single parents like her.

Later, practically homeless and afraid, Precious filed for divorce so that she could get enough welfare benefits to care for her son. Her husband put up little resistance, as he had already developed a stronger relationship with heroin than he had to his family. He would keep close tabs on the two of them, though, so Precious felt uneasy almost every day. She feared that his stints in county jail would escalate to something more serious, which they eventually did, so she tried her best to keep David away from his father.

It was not long into his years at Valley View Elementary School that young David continued his fascination with dismantling items and putting them back together in unusual ways. In science class, he finished the simple labs with ease, then created experiments of his own. In art class, he fixed a pottery wheel with a makeshift tool he had fashioned from a ruler and a staple remover. Everyone loved this eager little boy, and David gravitated to the motley assortment of staff members there for the things his mother could not always provide: a clean, safe environment, a hot meal, books, and of course, attention.

Realizing that the constant moving from place to place would hurt her son, Precious tried her best to keep a roof over their heads. Eventually she reconnected with her slightly deranged father, and he moved the two of them into the beat-up two-bedroom mobile home he owned in the remote recesses of rural Licking Valley. At first, David was a little wary of Gramps. His shaggy appearance and gruff way of talking was intimidating. He was good-natured, though, and broke the barrier with his young grandson by whittling animal figures out of wood and teaching him about the great outdoors. Through his colorful stories, David learned about Gramps's hippie days traveling across the country, his adventures outsmarting "bad guys," and the communal living of the 60's. He cried openly whenever he spoke of David's grandmother, whom he referred to as the best woman who had ever lived. He admitted how hard it had been to go on without her, and that she was in his thoughts and heart every single day.

Empty Desk

Gramps was one of those military survivalists who preferred to live off the grid and often stayed in the woods in a cleverly camouflaged area that presented no evidence of human life. The mobile home was just something he had inherited from his parents, and as far as he was concerned, he could take it or leave it. And leave it he did—often for weeks at a time. It had heat and electricity only intermittently, and that was just fine with Gramps. He was happy to let Precious and young David live there so they could have a roof over their heads and at least a little distance from the sleazy ex-husband and his equally shady connections.

By the time he reached middle school, David was an exceptional presence in the school. His intellect and unassuming manner endeared him to just about everyone. It was David who could coach a first grader to enjoy reading; it was David who made the rounds with the janitor after hours; it was David who captured the prize for every spelling bee or essay contest. However, if it were not for the generosity of his teachers, he might never have had the clean white shirt for the choir concert or the three dollars for the field trip to the Columbus Zoo.

To look at the young David Martin, one would never guess the stories he could tell. He had expertly juggled two conflicting worlds to survive: an impressive academic one and another, much darker and more sinister. By age eleven, he had witnessed a murder, nearly frozen to death, been attacked by wolves, and even stolen supplies to keep his mother and himself alive. At times, he rigged the door of his school so that he could slip inside on nights when it was too dangerous or too cold to go home. And that was not even half of the story that led David Martin from survival in Newark, Ohio to his new life as Jordan Michaels in Greeley, Colorado.

The story of how he got the name Jordan Michaels, though, epitomized the string of broken promises that characterized David Martin's life. In David's middle school years, Michael Jordan emerged as the best basketball player the world had ever known. During one of those stretches when David was a squatter at the school, he picked up Jordan's biography. The world of fame, fortune, and success was so far removed from young David and his meager Ohio life that Michael Jordan became his fantasy friend. He read everything he could find on the athlete and discovered that Jordan had been cut from his junior high school basketball team. David imagined that if some once poor black kid could become the best basketball player the world had ever known, maybe he could make it too.

David had inherited his grandfather's uncanny eye for detail and keen ability to build and to fix things. David often dreamed of one day being able to construct massive buildings and offices, to design and build solar houses, and to make prisons more habitable. These were lofty goals for a middle schooler, and David realized even then that he needed a college education. He considered how no one expected Michael Jordan to succeed, so young David resolved to *be like Mike*.

Precious was proud of these goals, but at the same time realized how unequipped she was to keep him from dangers that lurked everywhere. In fact, at times they did not even have food or running water. Gramps was unstable and largely absent. Her limited income consisted of what she made cleaning houses for a handful of families in Granville, a more affluent community not far

Empty Desk

from Newark. Sometimes, she resorted to peddling a little pot or a few pills that she took from the homes that she cleaned. As middle school ended, Precious put her plan to leave Ohio into action. Fortunately, at that time, David had limited knowledge of how his father, recently released from jail again, had begun to take control of their lives. Precious Martin knew that disappearing was the only chance the two of them would have for a normal life.

Initially, David did not take the news that they were going to flee Ohio well. On one hand, he had a strong support system at school. Furthermore, he loved Gramps, although the old man rarely came around anymore and when he did, he was not the same man that David had come to know. On the other hand, at times David himself had fantasized about leaving, having already experienced a good deal of danger and neglect. Maybe a new start would be best.

In an effort to soothe David's anxiety, Precious promised her son that he could give himself a new name. "Just think, you can be anyone you want. We will get far away from here, and you can concentrate on school. I'll get a job and we'll have a great place to live. You won't have to worry anymore; I promise you." David looked at his mother's quivering lips, and told her, "I know exactly what name I want. From now on, call me Michael Jordan."

Precious immediately knew that a name like that would only draw attention to them, so she reluctantly but instantly broke the first of many promises. She patiently explained how they could have a better life far away from Ohio, but they would have to fly under the radar. Having a celebrity name would be a mistake.

Empty Desk

When she saw the disappointment in her son's face, she suggested that Jordan Michaels might be a great alternative. David thought briefly, and decided it was a good compromise. Before long he started thinking of himself as Jordan. The name seemed to fit.

He never knew exactly how his mother had been able to get the paperwork to prove their new identities. He only knew that one of the school counselors at Horace Greeley High School in Colorado had previously been an acquaintance of his mother and a regular customer of his father's extensive drug ring. In her old life, the counselor's expertise had been falsifying and stealing identities. His mother informed him that the counselor had no desire to reveal her own jaded past, and that they would be safe hundreds of miles away from Newark, Ohio. Precious Martin (now Judith Michaels) had learned early that keeping a few secrets could lead to owing favors, and so she called this one in.

Head counselor Mrs. Linda Martino had no idea that one of her colleagues had created a fake birth certificate and transcripts for the new enrollee Jordan Michaels. It was a full month into the new school year, and Mrs. Martino cautioned both the student and his mother that he would have to make up all the work that he had missed. She welcomed them to the community, handed them the welcome packet, collected the school fees, printed up Jordan's schedule, and sent them off with a student tour guide. The transition from life as David Martin to one as Jordan Michaels was complete and uneventful.

Nelly thought about everything she knew about Jordan Michaels, the complicated young man whose quiet actions had saved lives and changed the course of so many more. She recalled their many after-school sessions when he slowly revealed his many secrets. He asked her to promise to keep his story confidential, and Nelly had agreed. She had honored that vow, but she regretted that the quiet boy with the plain shirt and a soft voice would never get the recognition he so rightly deserved.

Chapter 10

Nelly

Nelly reached back into the hidden drawer.

She gingerly pulled out two ledgers of deposits and withdrawals. The first displayed neat entries in appropriate columns, initialed clearly *CAL* by her former principal, Calvin Lambert. It showed expenditures for new textbooks that the English department had never purchased, for field trips that had never been taken, for office supplies that no one had ever seen, and for new carpet for the teachers' lounge that had never been ordered. The ledgers represented the rather primitive accounting system from the early 80's, a time when the finances of the district were rarely audited.

The second showed withdrawals that aligned perfectly with the dates that Calvin Lambert and his financial secretary Bella had gone to Aspen for leadership training and later to the secondary school conference in California. The two often met behind closed doors and rumors of their possible love affair had circulated for months. Nelly did not care what the two of them chose to do. What she did care about was the fact that the English department had not received the meager resources they needed to do their jobs.

Ironically, Principal Lambert had assigned Nelly to head the Budget Priority Committee, and it was her charge to convene a group of five staff members to recommend how to spend discretionary funds the following school year. These committees were the brainchild of a superintendent who wanted to promote the illusion that the administration and the teachers functioned collaboratively. Nelly accepted her assignment reluctantly, only slightly relieved that she had not been relegated to the school morale team or even worse, CSAP testing.

Her first order of business was to inspect the records of the current year, and this request had led to her acquisition of the files she now held in her hands. She had stopped by the office on a day that both Bella Evans and Calvin Lambert were out of town attending an administrative retreat.

A shy young substitute secretary, eager to please the staff, granted Nelly access to Lambert's office to retrieve the files. "Please do not remove any files. I will be happy to copy whatever you need for your committee," she declared.

Lambert was something of an obsessive-compulsive, so within minutes of scanning his meticulously labeled files, Nelly located what she would need. She handed the folder to the secretary, who later copied its contents and placed them in Nelly's mailbox. She did not even look at them for several weeks, but when she did, the realization of Lambert's indiscretions could not have been more transparent. She knew that what she had discovered had serious implications and she momentarily considered pitching the files.

After all, Lambert was far from the worst principal that Horace Greeley High School had hired. Nelly found him to be an articulate and passionate leader, someone who cared about kids and trusted teachers to use their own best judgment. The fact that he might be involved with

Empty Desk

Bella, who was married to an abusive alcoholic, was not Nelly's business. Besides, Bella was always the kindest and most welcoming of the entire front office staff, and the only time Nelly had met Bella's husband Mark, she found him a foul-mouthed and loathsome creature.

Nelly knew, though, that Lambert was himself married to an attractive young woman and they were raising a couple of elementary-aged kids. She had seen the whole family at the Friday night football games, with Lambert proudly hoisting his young sons into the air whenever the Coyotes scored a touchdown.

At the time, instead of returning or pitching the files, Nelly decided to take them home to inspect them more carefully, a task that ultimately revealed that funds for the English department's missing computer lab had been used to support several trips to mountain resorts or out-of-state conferences for her principal and his secretary.

She realized the tandem files had never been meant for her eyes; had Lambert not been so detail-oriented and the substitute secretary so trusting, Nelly would never have had any idea that they existed. Yet she had made the discovery, and this was a fraud that deeply impacted both the English Department and the students themselves. It is one thing to cheat on a spouse, but quite another to steal to make it happen. After taking the weekend to carefully consider her options, she decided to bet on Lambert's basic decency to do the right thing.

She scheduled a private appointment with him on a Friday afternoon, a time she knew that they could meet undisturbed and that the staff would have undoubtedly fled to prepare for the big game or stop off for a few beers at Pappy's Pub. He greeted her cheerfully and indicated she should take a seat.

Remembering her love of a good cup of coffee, he poured her a cup, and urged her to sit down. She did, and within minutes, they chatted comfortably about the state of the school. When the time was right, Nelly extracted the two ledgers from her notebook. She set them side-by-side on his desk. His reaction, though controlled, was immediate and intense.

"Where did you get these?" he demanded.

"Your substitute secretary copied them for me so that I could prepare my committee report. Remember? You put me in charge of the Budget Committee. I assure you that I am the only person who has seen them, and I am certain the sub just refiled the originals. I have only one concern. Remember when you and Bella attended that week-long leadership conference in Aspen last year? I believe that was about the same time that we were supposed to get the English Department's computer lab up and running."

Lambert faced flushed and he pulled anxiously on his ear. Before he could say anything, Deann suggested, "Perhaps it would be best to have that in place *before* we plan next year's budget. With that $25,000 for computers, we should be able to get the project off to a great start, and as you know, it is long overdue."

Cal Lambert took a hard look at Deann Nelson and weighed his options. He could make her life miserable, maybe even transfer her to the alternative school. He could call her bluff, shred the offending documents, and pretend this meeting had never occurred. Or he could borrow to the limits on his credit cards and replace the money he had so foolishly spent. He tapped his feet nervously, took a deep breath, and gazed directly into the eyes of a hard-working teacher who had called him out. He knew she had the best interests of the school at heart, and he had all along planned to make good on what he had "borrowed."

Knowing his own future rested solely on her, he rolled the dice. "Deann, that project is long overdue. Let's make it happen. You and I. Give me 60 days and I am certain that the full funding will be available. Will that be acceptable?"

Deann Nelson took the file, which she had previously copied just in case she needed a spare, and handed it over to Lambert. He clutched the files to his chest while he tried to figure out what else to say. Deann stood up, extended her hand, smiled, and replied, "Yes, sir. That will be fine. Thank you. Have a great weekend."

She practically ran down the hall, pleased that the lab would come to fruition and that Lambert could work out his own complicated life without her interference. It was enough that she had the proof in case he reneged on his pledge.

A few weeks before spring break that year, the local newspaper featured Ms. Deann Nelson and Mr. Calvin Lambert at the ribbon-cutting ceremony heralding the opening of the first computer laboratory in the Greeley public schools. There was a good deal of hand shaking and praise for the great progress in technology for Horace Greeley High School.

A few years later, the school's secretary Bella Evans divorced her husband Mark, quit her job, and returned to college to study optometry. That same year, Calvin Lambert, armed with a lucrative contract as the new assistant superintendent in a neighboring district, stopped by to tell Ms. Nelson goodbye.

"It has been an honor to serve with you, Deann. I owe you plenty. This is my last day here, Deann, so I just wanted to tell you thank you."

Deann smiled, crossed the room, and held out her hand. "Best wishes to you. You have been a great principal to work for. Congratulations on your new job. And on that new baby. Tell your wife that I hope she enjoys her new home."

"I will," Lambert said, "I will." He stepped out of the room and left the building. At the time, Deann thought about pulling the files from the secret drawer and destroying them, but before she could do so, the fire alarm had gone off, so they had remained in the secret drawer until now.

I can destroy these now, Nelly thought. She placed them in her getaway bag and resolved to shred them as soon as she got home.

Chapter 11

Jordan

Ms. Nelson stayed after school one wintry afternoon trying to make a dent in the ever-present stack of ungraded papers. No matter how disciplined she tried to be, the pile multiplied like rabbits in the spring. Although she tried to maintain a consistent exercise regimen, time for personal exercise was limited due to a never-ending stream of paperwork. Sometimes her summer assignments required a decent amount of military stamina, so she resolved to do better. She sighed, picked up her favorite fine-line red pen, and pulled the first essay off the top of the stack.

She glanced out the window, spotting Jordan Michaels with his threadbare jacket and gloveless hands shivering in the parking lot. Those days, the rule was simple: once the last bell rang for the day, unless students had a bona-fide appointment with a teacher, they had to get out of the building and stay out. The latest union contract prohibited the principal from requiring hall supervision beyond the school day, and he was not about to let teenagers have access to anything inside that could be stolen or broken.

Ms. Nelson observed Jordan for a while, then decided to invite him back into the building. No sense in witnessing a kid freeze to death. Besides, maybe she could learn a little more of his story. At that time, although Jordan trusted Ms. Nelson completely, he was still reticent to reveal too much. Theirs was a relationship that would span his four years of high school and beyond, but at this stage both were tentative about revealing too much of their personal lives.

Grateful for the warmth of the classroom, he glanced around to see if there was anything he could do to help his teacher. He spotted the broken desk that had been placed against the wall. Apparently, someone thought that loosening all the screws would lead to the ultimate demise of an unsuspecting student, and it had. To the initial delight of the Poetry class, Mary Dawson had tumbled to the floor with a heavy thud and a blood-curdling scream a few days earlier. Her fall had resulted in a fractured wrist, bruises, a frantic call from parents, not to mention a huge collection of paperwork documenting the event. The assistant principal, much more concerned about a potential lawsuit than Mary's condition, had warned Nelly to "keep a lid on the situation." Fortunately, all six of the Dawson kids had had Nelly as a teacher, and the parents seemed more concerned about Mary missing too much class than her injuries.

The desk frame was slightly bent now, and the top tray no longer connected to the chair. Nelly had covered it with masking tape and posted a *Danger* sign. She knew a repair would require a work order and three signatures, and she had not had time to do it. Her classes were packed, though, and she needed that desk.

Jordan wandered over to the wreckage and sized it up quickly. "Want me to fix this?" he asked. "I don't have any tools," Ms. Nelson explained. "No problem. I have a few," said Jordan. He reached into his multi-purpose backpack; he quickly unearthed a Philip's head screwdriver and some other tool that Ms. Nelson had never seen before. She returned to the dreadful prose of her composition class, while Jordan expertly assessed the damaged desk. Within a few minutes, he declared the desk "a goner." The frame was beyond repair.

"Want me to get you another desk? Mr. Ackerson never needs all of his." Ms. Nelson knew that was likely true. Ackerson was close to retirement and decided to spend his last few years making an "A" a near impossibility. With mounting pressure for strong GPA's, the exodus from his classes was palpable. Nelly contemplated the hassle of inventory sheets and requisition forms. The thought of bypassing the paperwork and the required signatures needed for approval of a work order pleased her.

"Jordan, I would love that. Think you can pitch this one in the dumpster and grab a good desk from Mr. Ackerson's room? It would have to be on the QT."

Jordan grinned. It was clear he should ask no questions, and he quickly grabbed the damaged desk and slipped out of the classroom. Within what seemed like seconds he was back with a sturdy replacement. He set it carefully in the correct row, then deftly tightened the screws on all the other desks.

"Thanks, Jordan. Where did you learn to be so handy?"

A quick smile crossed Jordan's face. "My grandpa taught me; that guy could fix anything. He was a great fisherman, too. Oh, and he could hunt like nobody's business."

"Do you get to see him often? Where does he live?"

"Um, he died. That bastard killed him." The joy drained from his face, as Jordan immediately realized he had revealed too much. He glanced out the window. "My mom is outside. I gotta go. Thanks for letting me come in." He stuffed his tools in his backpack, grabbed his jacket, and raced out of the room. It would be months before Ms. Nelson would learn the full story of the murder Jordan had witnessed.

After glancing nervously at his surroundings, Jordan climbed into the beat-up black pickup in the parking lot and it roared away. Ms. Nelson tried to digest what she had just learned from him, and then made a mental note to try to find a warm jacket for Jordan from the local Goodwill or on sale somewhere. He would not be the first student that she had supplied with clothing. She decided to ask him to repair a few more items before returning to the stack of essays that seemed to have grown exponentially.

She pondered what she already knew about Jordan: a grandpa who had been killed, a backpack of tools, and an assumed name. His would be a complex and amazing story. She was sure of it.

Chapter 12

Nelly

Nelly reached into the drawer to retrieve a colorful photograph that immediately brought a flood of joyful memories. The picture was slightly little faded now, but the twenty or so students with their bright smiles radiated like stars from its two-dimensional borders.

This was the only remaining tangible evidence of Nelly's Public Speaking class of 1985, and she was thrilled to have a reminder of this wonderful group of young people. The entire semester with them had been special, but on one extraordinary class period that year, this class generated one of those unexplained and treasured experiences recounted for years and relived at every class reunion. On that day, contagious laughter catapulted out of room 203, down the hallway, into the adjoining corridors, reaching far into the library and labs, gyms and offices.

It all started with an assignment that Nelly used to help students overcome their fear of public speaking. After observing her students for a few days at the start of the semester, Nelly had an accurate sense of which students might like the spotlight, those who would power through the course because they needed it for graduation, and those who were terrified beyond belief. She resolved that every single one of them would make it through the course.

She decided to have each student demonstrate a way **not** to give a speech. She wrote the descriptions on notecards, instructed the class that they had to meet just three criteria: speak for a full 90 seconds, talk about a memorable experience, and exaggerate the fault. She explained that getting an "A" on the first speech would be easy—the speech was supposed to be horrible. She instructed them to prepare the assignment for the next day and to use any notes they wished. She had realized early in her career that for many students the textbook's *Autobiography of My Life* speech was too intrusive, sometimes even painful. Not everyone wanted to share the fact that their mom was in prison or that they did not have enough money to pay the electric bill. This was a lot less stressful. She then carefully distributed the descriptions, matching the students with her early perceptions of them.

She handed *Silent Speaker* to Melissa, a painfully shy young woman whose hands shook when she received her challenge. Her instructions were to speak barely above a whisper and act as if she could barely stand to look at her audience, a task that she accepted with great relief. To the resident artist, ironically named Art, she handed the task of *Chalkboard Freak*. His challenge fit perfectly: to speak with passion to the chalkboard rather than the audience and graphically illustrate every point. Gabby got *Note Card Reader*; her task was to read everything word-for-word, and in the process complain about not being able to make out the words on the cards. Added to these were a couple dozen more: *The Scratcher, The Pointer, The Pauser, The Pacer, The Klutz, The Brown Noser*, and others.

Nelly could not have anticipated just how well she had matched these students with their skills and how much fun the next class would be. She realized as she gazed at the photo that it was one of those experiences that could never be duplicated or explained. It was just magic, a time when all the variables and complexities and angst of adolescence combined into something truly unforgettable.

The class began with the assistant principal's customary public-address announcements about campus cleanliness, the time change for a Key Club meeting, and the upcoming basketball tournament. Then they all stood and recited the *Pledge of Allegiance*. After these preliminaries were over, in a not-so-subtle attempt to delay their own speeches, one of Nelly's former students demanded, "Whoaaaa, Nelly, tell us a story first." By this time, Nelly's storytelling had become legendary, and she was used to having an early-in-the-semester tale or two to engage her class.

So, to demonstrate what she expected from her students, Nelly revealed one of her own early school experiences, a time when she violated a school rule about not chewing gum. Her punishment, administered by her former eighth-grade English teacher, a Dominican nun named Sister Mary Theodora, was to wear a chewed-up wad of gum on her nose for the duration of the school day. At lunch, even after the gum fell into her mashed potatoes and gravy, Sister Theodora insisted that she retrieve it and put it back on her nose.

One tale led to another, and the class was delighted to think that their own teacher had suffered some of the same indignities that they had. They found it hard to believe that students actually held out their hands to be whacked with rulers, that boys were sent home for not wearing ties, or that girls had to avoid patent leather shoes since they could reflect their underpants. Although Nelly had both hated and dreaded her days in Catholic school, she was later grateful for the many stories it generated.

The class was clearly on a roll, distracted from concerns of football games and SAT tests, alcoholic fathers and essay deadlines; when they began to present their own "horrible" speeches, it became almost a competition to see just how bad they really could be.

Melissa was one of the early presenters, and when she could barely squeak out a word, the class laughed; it was not a mean-spirited laugh, but one of genuine hilarity and affirmation.

Then it was Art's turn, and he took out the colored chalk and began sketching huge diagrams of his elementary school classmates. His exaggerated movements made them laugh even more. After wiping his brow, his face and clothes became smeared in chalk dust, and the spectacle got even funnier.

One by one, they made their way to the front of the room. With every speech, each nuance and misstep was accompanied by the thunderous laughter of a fully engaged audience. As Jerry talked about summer camp, he frantically paced back and forth like an expectant father; Martha's explanation of a trip to the dentist was accompanied by an incessant series of "ums" and "ahs" delivered in a whiny pitch; Tom did a face plant on his way to the front of the room, spilling all the props he had brought with him to demonstrate his first fishing trip; Jim sprayed his cheeks with water as he cried crocodile tears when telling a sad story about a pet cricket dying.

Nelly glanced around the room, pleased that for the previous hour every single student had been actively involved in the day's lesson. However, nothing could have prepared them for what came next.

Empty Desk

Alex had requested to use a hall pass a little earlier, and he returned with a smirk on his face and a spring in his step. He was a total charmer, a loveable young man, but one who had endured his fair share of bullying, often because of his 350-pound frame. He had drawn the fault *Inappropriate Dresser*, something that Nelly assumed would involve a T-shirt advocating beer consumption of something of that sort.

Instead, Alex lumbered up to the front of the room in his usual sweatpants and tee shirt. He started telling about his first swim lessons, and how he feared the water. For the first time that morning, the speaker did not provoke the amusement that had characterized the previous presentations. Alex sensed the class expected a little more, and he aimed to please.

He informed the audience that he needed to demonstrate his first venture into the water. He removed his sweatshirt and the massive rolls of fat jiggled slightly. Not wanting to offend him, the class at first contained their laughter. But once he dropped his sweatpants and stood there in a miniscule Speedo, barely detectable under the rolls of flesh, they erupted into a laughter avalanche. With a grin that stretched to heaven, Alex stood on tip toes, then bent over to demonstrate his first dive into the swimming pool. His theatrics conveyed that it was perfectly okay to be amused, and he himself howled like a pack of wolves on a desolate Colorado mountaintop.

One by one, the students shrieked with laughter, not really at Alex, but at the sheer enormity of every ridiculous thing life offered. As Alex got dressed again, the class laughed until tears streamed down their faces in tiny rivers and once the frenzy subsided, it rose once again.

Empty Desk

Mr. Weberlein stepped out from his classroom across the hall because he became concerned over the commotion. "Is everything OK?" he asked, and the shrieks began again. He scratched the three remaining hairs on the top of his head and clicked his heels before turning to leave. "I am going to open my classroom door," he declared, "because it is obviously more fun in here."

He returned to his Algebra students, but when the joy of Room 203 reverberated across the hall, his students started laughing too. They did not know how or why they laughed, only that they had no control over it. One classroom door after another opened and a few of Ms. Nelson's colleagues stepped out into the hallway to marvel at the jubilation emanating from Room 203. The sounds were so foreign, so unexpected, and so irresistible that even the resident crab Mr. Barr took a moment to listen before returning to his room with a rather paltry "Humppffff!"

No teachers closed their classroom doors, not even when Principal Ford strutted purposely down the hallway to ferret out the source of all the racket. Before he even reached Room 203, he sensed it had to be another issue with Ms. Nelson, a teacher who had trouble following rules. She hung weird pictures on the walls, besieged him with field trip requests, paraded her students out in the rain, asked questions at faculty meetings, and even invited ex-cons and the elderly to her room to "tell stories." He tolerated her, though, because she seldom referred students to the administration and would often take students no one else wanted.

He fixed a stern expression on his face and peered into the classroom. "Why all the hullabaloo in here?" he asked. As soon as the word "hullabaloo" rolled off his lips, the collective laughter absolutely exploded. Ms. Nelson stood up from her seat at the back of the room to explain, but as soon as she did, she collapsed into convulsions of laughter. For a moment she thought she might pee her pants. The class had never seen anyone, and definitely never a teacher, lose control in such an unorthodox way. To do so in front of the principal made it even more remarkable. The spectacle caused them to do the only thing they could: erupt into another laughing frenzy.

Ford wanted to exert his dominance and put an end to the nonsense, but something about the whimsy of the joy echoing down the halls made him put his hands in his pockets and head back to his office without a word. Once he got there, he glanced at his secretary with her bright red lipstick and gigantic hooped earrings. Something about the way those earrings dangled struck him as incredibly funny. He gulped and then did something he had never done before or since: he let out a belly laugh. It was such an unfamiliar, unexpected sound that Miss Dawson immediately snickered, and the student aide Contessa began to giggle.

Within minutes, the entire office staff started laughing, at first just a few suppressed giggles but later spasms of laughter that took on a life of their own. Strange outbursts like these continued throughout the entire day. No one really knew what was funny or why, but that day no one questioned why Coach Potter sang happily in the mailroom or what caused Mrs. McIntire to skip into her classroom or even why Mr. Conner, the normally quiet and stoic parking lot attendant, whistled the entire afternoon. When the day ended, and students and staff headed home uncharacteristically upbeat and smiling, they knew intuitively that they had experienced a special once-in-a-lifetime event. When they tried to explain it, people just shook their heads and dismissed it.

Nelly smiled, grateful for the chance to have been a part of that one incredible day. *I will frame this photo*, she thought, as she carefully packed it away.

Chapter 13

Jordan

One afternoon Nelly learned a little more about Jordan's mother and their adjustment to Colorado. She sat quietly, just listening, as Jordan revealed his devotion to his mom.

Precious Martin made the transition to Judith Michaels rather seamlessly. Her forged credentials, and those of her son, were superb, and her commitment to her son's education and safety was all the motivation she needed to cut ties with Ohio. She resolved to put her past indiscretions, an abusive ex-husband, the death of her parents, and other painful personal memories in the rear-view mirror.

When the two members of the new "Michaels" family first arrived in Greeley, Colorado, they rented a one-bedroom apartment in a run-down, but relatively safe section of town. Judith and Jordan had surmised correctly that they would not be scrutinized too carefully in this location. Fortunately, the current owner was not concerned in the least about Judith's past or that of her kid. After she offered to pay six months' rent in advance, he simply jotted down her name, the fake previous address she provided, and a disconnected phone number. He handed her the keys, assured her that the apartment was all ready for occupancy, and then headed to the local tavern. She had not expected things to go so easily; she took the new living arrangements as a good omen, and allowed some of her uneasiness to subside.

Empty Desk

With the help of a few trips to Target, Judith quickly transformed their 800 square foot apartment into a comfortable and welcoming living space. A few cozy lavender cushions and a plush purple floor rug made a big difference. Jordan pulled out his tools and got to work customizing the closet with an impressive collection of cubby holes, shelves, and hooks, allowing ample room for their meager possessions.

The two of them marveled at hot water being readily available day or night; Judith found herself switching the lights on and off, satisfied that the electricity was fully functioning. Jordan used a level to precisely hang some pictures of lilies at eye level. When they saw the results of their efforts, they both felt like they finally had a real home. Not that they would be welcoming visitors any time soon.

Both Judith and Jordan had promised each other to stick to their stories of a previous life in Saginaw, Michigan. They selected Saginaw because Jordan had done a report on it in middle school; the city had deteriorated so much from the closing of the General Motors factories that there was not much left of it. Judith intended to list a defunct Saginaw beauty supply shop as her previous employment; if a potential employer tried to check out her story, he would find that the phone number she supplied had been disconnected. Jordan's forged transcripts would show an unimpressive academic record at St. Mary's, a school that had recently closed.

Jordan was just a freshman when they arrived in Greeley, but he already had greater wisdom and maturity than his mother would ever have. He assured his mother that he would not bring anybody home, that he would stick to himself at school. Although Jordan did not know all the details about his father's crimes and his parents' ominous drug connections, he knew enough to convince himself of the need to stay below the radar.

Whether it was due to his intellect or his extensive reading of crime stories, Jordan thought of details his mother would never have even considered. They would wear generic Target clothes. No Nikes that someone would notice and comment upon, no jewelry that would interest anyone, no flashy colors that would in any way make them conspicuous, and definitely no Ohio Buckeye sweatshirts. They would keep an unlisted phone number, and they would never, ever contact anyone from Newark, Ohio.

Precious Martin got used to being called Judith. She and Jordan had practiced using their new names in practically every sentence they spoke on the first leg of their trip from Ohio; by the time they left their stopover location in Nebraska, both embraced their new identities. Judith promised herself and her son to remain vigilant. She was proud of having made it this far into a new life, and she did not want to do anything to screw it up.

For a while, while Jordan was away at school, she mostly stayed inside, filling her days with re-runs of *CSI* and *48 Hours*. She considered what it might be like to work in law enforcement, helping people like herself who found themselves in impossible situations. She knew deep down that would be unlikely, but still held out hope that at least Jordan would find a career path that he would love.

Before their first year in Greeley had passed, Judith got bored of the crime shows and *Jerry Springer* episodes, and she decided to find a job. She and Jordan talked at length about where to look. Restaurants might be fine, but tips were undependable, and they did not offer any medical insurance. Gas stations were sketchy, and Jordan did not want his mother working long into the night. The banks and big cable companies would undoubtedly scrutinize her documents closely. She had no marketable skills to speak of; except for cleaning a few houses and selling some pot, her employment history was non-existent.

After rejecting just about every possibility, they agreed that Walmart might be the perfect solution. The store nearby was currently hiring, offered medical insurance after 90 days of full-time employment, and granted an employee discount. Jordan figured that they were not likely to investigate their associates too thoroughly, as he had read that even illegals could get work there. Judith had already successfully acquired a Colorado driver's license, and with that and a few other convincing documents, she would likely pass their cursory inspection.

Within a week after she applied, Judith was pinning on her Walmart name tag and making the short drive to work. For some time, she worked as a floater, moving from department to department to fill in where needed. This was fortunate, as she did not need to bond with co-workers much and no one seemed particularly interested in her background. A lot of her fellow workers were like Judith, not particularly skilled, and often transplanted from other areas of the country. Many, like her, were single parents doing their best to get by. Most kept to themselves, and this suited Judith just fine.

Her pay was minimum wage, but at first Judith was thrilled to even have a job. Before long, though, the novelty wore off and she started to compare the meager funds she earned to what the managers made. She was a decent worker, and the managers recognized that early, often assigning her tasks they did not want to do. However, as she approached the 90-day mark and their eligibility for insurance, the Human Resources office started scheduling her for fewer hours. To get the insurance, she needed to maintain an average of 36 hours. She was scheduled for only 32. It was a typical corporate ploy big companies like Walmart used to avoid paying benefits to their employees, and Judith fumed. It was not the first time in her life that she had been at someone else's mercy, and she felt helpless about changing the situation.

As a result, Judith's initial work ethic waned a bit, and she began to entertain herself by watching the people of Walmart. She detected a few shoplifters, several of them employees, but decided to ignore them. Most were not very good at it anyway, and eventually got spotted by store security. Judith figured that she had seen her own share of hard times, and considering what they were paid, Walmart deserved to take the hit.

Over time, Judith boredom increased. There were just so many times that she could sort returns, count how many packages of granny panties were on the racks, and clean a disgusting restroom before she started to question her sanity. She reminded herself, though, that one day Jordan would go to college and then land a dream job. Until then, she resolved to hang in there.

Chapter 14

Nelly

Nelly moved forward with her packing, reaching into the drawer with her eyes closed, eager to see what other memory awaited. This time she grasped a small gift bag containing two apples, one an intricately hand-carved wooden creation, the other a rather gaudy but expensive gold version, gifts from parents of her former students, Julian Cordova and Kathy Fillmore. They had both graduated in 1991 and their journeys could not have been more different.

Horace Greeley High School had a banner year in 1991, as this was the year that four seniors earned prestigious Boettcher scholarships, and the district was giddy over its role. These scholarships pretty much guaranteed recipients a promising future; each had a full ride for the entire four years and colleges were eager to lure such brilliant students to their campuses. Three of these kids had come to the district already armed with highly educated parents, unlimited travel experiences, academic tutors, and high IQ's, but one recipient, the steadfast Julian Cordova, had managed to grab the coveted prize despite a life of poverty and struggle.

Graduation day that year had been particularly exquisite. Blue skies punctuated with piercing white clouds and balmy temperatures put the crowd in a festive mood. *Pomp and Circumstance* floated majestically above the audience followed by the customary speeches filled with platitudes and lofty aspirations. Touching vocal solos and tearful good-byes highlighted the ceremony, ending with

Empty Desk

Superintendent Alfano providing a boring recital of the many accomplishments of the district, noting the large number of Boettcher scholarship winners in a tribute far more flattering to himself than the students who had earned them.

After the ceremony concluded and their teacher duties were completed, Nelly and her colleagues left to head to graduation parties to which they had been invited. Most of the faculty looked forward to meeting their students' families, and these teachers had more than earned every lunch, glass of wine, or thank-you note that would characterize the day.

Every year Nelly wrestled with whether to bring a gift, generally opting not to do so; most of the teachers were barely getting by themselves so a thoughtful card would have to suffice. She also chose to go solo to the gatherings, preferring the flexibility to move on at her own pace. Besides, although she got along well her colleagues, she did not belong to any of the teacher cliques, which were every bit as common as those among the high school students themselves.

Nelly inspected the stack of party invitations in her purse before deciding to start with Kathy Fillmore's event. Kathy was a Boettcher scholar and all-around good kid, and one of Nelly's favorites. Nelly knew Kathy came from immense wealth, but she was unprepared for the spectacle of her party. The setting was her grandparents' ranch, just outside the city limits. Acres of carefully groomed fields hugged the professionally landscaped grounds of the estate's mansion. The interior featured sparkling chandeliers, ornate flowing fountains, and strange, exotic artwork. Nelly strolled among the guests as violinists in tuxedoes performed and properly trained wait staff served baked oysters in half shells, prawn kebobs, and exotic goat cheeses.

Nelly immediately felt her middle-class status as soon as the perfectly manicured, elegantly attired Mrs. Thomas Fillmore III swept over to greet her. Feeling conspicuous with her shabby fingernails and simple black dress, Nelly regretted not wearing the high heels she reserved for special occasions, having decided at the last minute to be comfortable rather than stylish. She tried to shrug aside her discomfort and prepared to greet her host.

"It is so nice to see you again, Mrs. Fillmore. You must be so proud of Kathy."

"Call me Madeline," Mrs. Fillmore cooed. "I am so pleased you were able to come. Kathy always speaks so highly of you. Yes, we are definitely proud of our daughter. I hope you are hungry; please enjoy some food. Our chef promised us something special today, and I am certain he will not disappoint. Also, please take one of the gift bags we have specially prepared for Kathy's wonderful teachers. They are over in the foyer."

Nelly smiled and started to say something more about Kathy, but her hostess pirouetted left to welcome her more prestigious guests. Over the years Nelly had often felt the social class divide between the wealthy families of Weld County and middle and lower classes like herself. Although many parents were gracious and grateful, they nevertheless conveyed that they regarded teachers as something akin to hired help. Abandoned, Nelly strolled over to the foyer and glanced at the gallery of photos of the family's Arabian horses; they featured Kathy proudly riding her personal horse Morning Glory, one they had somehow arranged to be shipped to the United States from Saudi Arabia. Despite the extravagant wealth, Kathy had turned out to genuinely kind and down to earth, but one glance around these surroundings made it abundantly clear that Kathy did not need a scholarship; this family could fund a college education and then some.

"Ms. Nelson, MS. NELSON, I am so glad you are here," shrieked Kathy as soon as she spotted her favorite teacher. The two shared a brief hug, and Nelly offered her congratulations. Kathy thanked her profusely for the letters of recommendation she had written on her behalf. Then she grabbed Nelly's hand. "Please, come outside with me. I want to introduce you to my horse Morning Glory."

The teacher followed her happy student out to the stable where the majestic stallion tossed his head carelessly as the sun gleamed against his glistening body. Kathy and the horse obviously had a deep bond, and Nelly wondered how they would manage without one another when Kathy headed to Princeton in the fall. She glanced around the stable itself, which was something of a spectacle. Fully supplied with cooling fans, ample feed, sweeping awnings, and expansive rooms for horses to interact with one another, the area was far grander than most people's living spaces. After the brief tour and an explanation of dressage, Nelly told Kathy to go enjoy her party. She gave her student an impulsive hug and wished her well, letting her know that she had a few more graduation parties to attend.

On her way out, Nelly picked up one of the teachers' gift bags. The contents included a $25 Starbuck's gift card, an engraved ink pen, and the gold apple that Nelly now held in her hands. She had never really used it in any way but kept it because it contrasted so starkly with the second apple, a wooden masterpiece intricately carved by the disabled father of Julian Cordova. In some ways, these two gifts, one likely paid for with a corporate credit card and the other fashioned by the crippled hands of an illegal immigrant, epitomized Nelly's entire career. Kathy's and Julian's stories could not have been more divergent, yet Nelly believed that both would become spectacular adults.

As she drove to the seedy outskirts of Greeley to attend Julian's party, her senses heightened to the potential dangers for a white woman traveling alone deep into the heart of the Latino community. Here and there were splotches of color, often bright reds and turquoise, but if it were not for the lush trees and bushes from a particularly rainy May, this was a neighborhood of despair. One did not have to look far to spot the rusted carcasses of abandoned vehicles, the discarded cigarette butts, the sagging steps and porches, or the menacing expressions of the occasional person on the street.

It took a while for Nelly to find the tattered apartment building that was home for Julian, his seven siblings, and his handicapped father. Julian had written a paper about his family for Senior English, so Nelly already knew that his mother had died while giving birth to her eighth child and that his father had been severely injured in an industrial accident. She knew that Mr. Cordova had signed a legal document absolving an Arizona oil company from further liability for his injuries; at the time he spoke no English and did not understand the agony that would characterize the rest of his life; because he was illegally in the United States, his sole focus was on keeping his large family stateside, and signing the document enabled him to do just that.

Empty Desk

Nelly sized up the apartment building and headed for number 8. Before she got close enough to knock, she could already hear the loud salsa music and the chatter of conversations in Spanish. She rang the doorbell rather tentatively, vaguely nervous about intruding on what must be a triumphant personal family celebration. In the entire history of the Cordova family, no one had ever graduated, let alone entertained the thought of college. Yet Julian had surpassed all the odds and he too would soon be part of a select group of Boettcher winners to attend the highly-respected Colorado College.

A small brown face with enormous charcoal eyes peeked through the blinds and immediately lit up. "THE TEACHER IS HERE! THE TEACHER IS HERE!" she screamed.

Several seconds passed before the door opened to what appeared to be twenty little kids, all screaming and jumping and shouting "Teacher."

Nelly smiled, then spotted the handsome Julian, who hustled over, hand outstretched, to greet her. "I am so happy you are here, Ms. Nelson. So happy." A glance at the beaming smile plastered across his face told his teacher just how much he meant it. "Come meet my father; he was hoping that you would come," he urged.

Julian led his teacher through the cramped apartment and out to the courtyard where he found his father, a once strong figure who now stood scarred and withered in front of her. Mr. Cordova turned to face the teacher who had recognized how important it would be for Julian to stay in school rather than drop out to work more hours to help support the family. Somehow, the family had managed to survive, and no one could be prouder of this

Boettcher scholar than Mr. Cordova himself. "My son," he said, "My son is going to college; he is going to be a doctor." He said it with the authority befitting the head of a strong and honorable family, one whose roots stretched back to his ancient ancestors.

When he faced Ms. Nelson, he dropped respectfully to his knees and grasped her hands. His eyes brimmed with tears and in a halting voice, he declared, "Gracias, muchisimas gracias. Usted ayudó a mi niño. Que Dios me la bendiga." Ms. Nelson flushed with emotion, particularly when the dozens of excited girls and boys in their best Sunday clothes gathered around her in a reverent hush. They sensed the significance of the moment and clapped delightedly.

At that second, Nelly realized that this was her red-carpet moment, and that no Emmy could compare to the majesty of this simple gesture. She was truly touched by the kneeling figure in front of her and had to contain the catch in her throat.

Just then a spectacular mariachi band appeared, heralding the start of the meal and the toasts. The sounds of trumpets blended exquisitely with velvety baritones as Mr. Cordova struggled to his feet, took her arm, and led her to the head table, beautifully decorated with multi-colored fruits and flowers. He indicated she was to sit in the place of honor, then took the microphone from the lead singer.

The crowd turned their attention to Julian's father and listened intently as he led them in prayer. "Señor, gracias te damos por todas las bendiciones que hemos recibido. Gracias por poner en nuestro camino a esta maestro que tanto nos ha ayudado y por darnos la Fortaleza para perseverar ante la adversidad."

Empty Desk

After a hearty chorus of *amens*, Mr. Cordova told the story of Julian's journey. At times the words came out in a clumsy combination of Spanish and English; at others they flowed seamlessly in the strong and steady cadence of his native tongue.

Finally, he reached into a small brown bag that had been carefully hidden beneath the table and pulled out the figure of a stallion that he had chiseled precisely from a precious piece of cherry wood. This was no ordinary stallion; it was a glorious creature with a streaming mane, passionate eyes, and inordinate grace. The crowd gazed in amazement at the gift and listened quietly as he urged his son to come forward.

Mr. Cordova cleared his throat, and with tears glistening on his wrinkled cheeks, he offered it to his son, "From the time you were small, you always wanted a horse. This is something we could never afford, and I always hoped that one day I could give you a real horse. This was not to be, but I hope you will take this one and know that it was the very best I could do to help give you your dream. I am proud of you, son, and your mama would be too."

Nelly struggled to contain her emotions, flashing back briefly to the spacious grounds of the Fillmore estate and the very real Morning Glory. She could not help but note the even greater value of the intricately carved figure before her. Julian raced over to embrace his proud father. "This **is** my dream horse, Papa. Thank you."

It was then time for the feast to begin. Nelly could hardly wait to try the hot salsas, fresh mangos, and cheesy burritos smothered with guacamole. But the Cordova family had a surprise for "the teacher." The mariachi band blasted the trumpets once more and Julian's sister

Empty Desk

Maria came waltzing to the table with a sizzling steak on an ornate platter.

"We did not know if you would like Mexican food, so my father cooked this especially for you," she said, flashing a beautiful smile. At first, Nelly began to protest, but then realized what this steak must have cost and how thoughtfully they must have planned this. "Thank you, thank you," she said softly.

"We have a gift for you too, Ms. Nelson," said Mr. Cordova. "I hope you will like it. No es mucho, but I have carved an apple especially for you. See, it has a seed, a seed like the one you planted in my son. It has a stem, like the one from which my son has grown. Como las ideas que usted sembróen mi hijo. Gracias, señora, gracias." Ms. Nelson tenderly touched the apple and savored the hot, salty tears that coursed down her cheeks.

The parallel lives of Kathy Fillmore and Julian Cordova had rarely intersected, but the stories of their journeys--symbolized by the real and fashioned horses and the bejeweled and wooden apples--were now part of Ms. Nelson's legacy.

Deann Nelson jolted herself from her reverie and continued packing up her life.

Chapter 15

Jordan

It was not long into Jordan's freshman year that he found himself wandering to Nelly's classroom whenever he had free time. Nelly did not mind, not only because he was such a well-mannered young man, but also because he willingly adjusted bulletin boards, hung mobiles from the ceiling, corrected the clock, or performed any other tasks she requested. She worried, though, that he appeared to have no friends, and he resisted her efforts in the classroom to ensure that he make a few. One day Nelly asked him about it.

"Do you like it here at Horace Greeley High School? You are doing well in your classes, but are you meeting good friends? Have you thought about joining Student Council or the Industrial Arts Club? You are so great with fixing things and solving problems. I bet these groups would love to have you join."

Jordan gave her a look bordering on the teenage eye roll and sneer, an act that delighted Nelly. It was encouraging to know that this serious young man had a "typical" side to him despite all the evidence pointing otherwise.

"Look, Ms. Nelson. I trust you, but I can't make friends. If I do, I will have to tell them about my life in Ohio, and that could put my mother and me in danger. She has a job here and everything. We have an apartment and Gramps's truck. We never had that before. I don't want to mess it up. After I get out of college, I am going to make sure my mom has a good life, and then I can have friends again. Besides, you know about the whole name thing."

That was not completely true. She knew his previous name and that this one had been invented, but she had yet to learn the full story. She decided to probe a little. She did not think the kid was in imminent danger but was curious to know more of his story.

"Jordan, help me understand. You do not have to reveal anything you do not want to, but it is not healthy for a kid to be alone all the time, to avoid extra-curricular activities. You are only in high school for a few short years, and you should be having some fun. Are you in some kind of danger?"

"No….yes….maybe. You see, my dad is in prison, at least I think he still is. My mom wanted to get me away from him and all his criminal friends, but she had no money and no skills to get me out of there. Gramps knew that she wanted out, so he arranged to help one of the big Ohio drug lords sell a particularly large shipment from Mexico. His cut would be enough to finance our escape; he told my mom it would be his gift to her for not really being a responsible parent when she was growing up."

Jordan paused, and then allowed the words to spill out, "The thing is, Gramps still had connections to my dad's former contacts, and figured correctly that they would be eager to get their hands on a way to make some easy money. To make things even more complicated, Gramps was very sick, and even though Mom tried to hide the fact from me, I still overheard enough to know that he would not live long.

Empty Desk

As old and as sick as he was, Gramps was still crafty, so he managed to get enough money out of the deal to finance us for a couple years or so. Then he got greedy and since he felt like he had nothing to lose, he pulled a fast one and kept every dime from moving the drugs, even the cut for the others involved. Some guy tracked Gramps down in the woods and shot him when he refused to tell him where the money was. I was there when it happened, but I was hiding in a lean-to and the shooter couldn't see me."

"I am so sorry, Jordan. That must have been terrible. Did you notify the police?"

"Hell, no. I mean, no. I waited like an eternity before I felt safe to move, then dragged Gramps's body to his hiding place, a kind of underground bunker out in the boonies. I headed back to the mobile home we were living in to tell my mom. It had been ransacked and everything torn apart, and I was so scared that they got to my mom too. She was there, but all beat up. She screamed and cried when she saw me. I told her about Gramps and she decided right then and there it was time to leave. We got into the truck and took off, and we headed for Nebraska that very night. That drug money was in a hidden compartment in the door of the truck. Gramps had fixed it so that no one could tell, which was a good thing because we when we left we did not take our clothes or food or anything with us."

"Do you have family in Nebraska?"

"No. Nebraska is on the way to Colorado, and Mom had already been planning this move for quite a while. We checked into a Holiday Inn in Kearney and hung out there for a few weeks until my mother got things fixed up here with the counselor. She told me not to ask too many questions about that; the less I knew, the better. We bought some new clothes at Target and some tires for the truck. I put the tires on myself so nobody would try to strike up a conversation or spot the place in the truck door where we kept the money. I still feel bad leaving Gramps buried out in the woods like that, and so did Mom. She told me that he would understand and if he were to pick a place to be buried, that his hideout in the woods would be it. She said that he would not have lived much longer and that getting us a new start was his legacy to us. He wanted me to just concentrate on getting on with my schooling in Colorado."

Nelly let some of the facts sink in then asked, "How did you get to enroll with a fake name?"

Jordan was short on details, but he admitted that his mother had a Greeley connection who was good at forging documents. Nelly decided not to pursue the issue further, a little wary of her own legal responsibilities to disclose these revelations. If one of her colleagues was helping Judith and Jordan, Nelly did not need to know.

Nelly probed a little more about Gramps and learned that he and Jordan's grandmother had lived the vagabond lifestyle of the 60's, sharing the road and communes with other pot smokers and war protestors of the time. Gramps discovered that he had inherited the Ohio land while making funeral arrangements for his mother, so that brought him back to the Midwest. Once his own wife died, he was so heartbroken that he considered suicide.

With no family or friends in Ohio, he became a recluse and a survivalist of sorts. He preferred his solitude and the great outdoors. He had little interest in the ramshackle mobile home on the property, preferring a well-camouflaged underground bunker he had constructed far into the woods. He subsisted primarily on wild mushrooms and berries that sprouted up along the creek beds and the occasional deer or small animal from hunting.

Gramps loved his daughter and grandson, but he was not the kind of man who wanted constant company. When the two of them moved into the dilapidated trailer on his property, they got the electricity running once again. Gramps rigged it with alarms and booby traps to alert them in case Jordan's dad returned or any other potential intruders surfaced. Then he pretty much disappeared into the woods for days at a time, leaving his rather immature daughter and resourceful grandson to fend for themselves.

Chapter 16

Nelly

Nelly picked up the thick folder containing her evaluations, carefully thumbing through the written reviews her supervisors had completed about her as an educator. She thought about the procession of principals who had led Horace Greeley High School over the years. Nelly grinned, then grimaced, thinking of the many stories this cast of characters had provided. Each one had arrived with a specific plan, some personal agenda to make this school distinctive, or in some cases, to make a name for themselves. Most were decent men--it was rare to find females in administrative posts--but several were so weak that the staff wondered how they had even gotten hired in the first place.

Many of them lasted for two or three years before moving on to a bigger high school, a more prestigious administrative position, or retirement. Some, like Lambert, left a decent legacy. Others faded into the recesses of Nelly's memory without even a beep on the radar. There were a few that Nelly would never forget. Saul Ford was one of these, and the purple cards Nelly pulled out of the drawer reminded her of his rather long tenure at Horace Greeley High School.

Dr. Ford considered himself a wordsmith. His solution to every problem was to construct a "correct" verbal response that was supposed to create immediate understanding and empathy in the listener. In Ford's reasoning, it was all about communication. "When we com-muuuun-i-catttttte," he would cajole, "we change the world."

If a student ever told a teacher to "fuck off," the teacher's scripted response had to be "I do not think you meant to say that. I can sense your frustration. Please rephrase your statement in a more appropriate way." If a parent wanted an update on a student's progress, the correct response had to be: "Please consult the online gradebook, which is updated daily. Once you have done so, I will be happy to set up a face-to-face meeting at your convenience."

In a relatively short time, every remark in the teachers' lounge was subject to translation.

"Good morning, Brandon."

"Don't you mean: Best wishes on this magnificent day of splendid instruction?"

"Screw you, Brandon. Can't someone just say good morning around here?"

"I do not think that your comment was meant the way you stated it. Perhaps you could rephrase it in a more pleasing way," smirked Brandon.

"By all means, Sir. How's this? I have a piece of jagged metal that I would enjoy pushing aggressively up your anal cavity."

After a few more pointed exchanges, the teachers would finish up their god-awful coffee, check their mailboxes, grin, and shuffle off to class.

Ironically, Saul Ford assumed that the well-educated teachers on his staff were incapable of being trusted to

Empty Desk

frame communication for themselves. To that end, he had created a series of translation cards for teachers to use, and he had them printed on purple paper with gold lettering to mirror the school's colors.

Nelly pulled a pack of these euphemisms from the secret drawer. She had saved them, not because they held any real value to her, but because she figured that some future teacher would never believe such instructions ever came from a real administrator without some proof. She scanned the card *What to Say at Parent-Teacher Conferences.*

Don't say this:	Say this:
Your son/daughter is stupid.	Your son/daughter has learning difficulties.
Your son/daughter cheats.	Your son/daughter has honesty issues.
Your son/daughter is rude.	Your son/daughter needs a little etiquette work.
Your son/daughter is lazy.	Your son/daughter needs a little motivation, which I will be happy to provide.
Your son/daughter does not get along with the other students.	Your son/daughter would benefit from a few more positive social interactions.
Your son/daughter is often tardy.	Your son/daughter would benefit from a little better time management.

Empty Desk

She could not suppress a belly laugh when saw the replacement card that her colleagues had written. Dr. Ford had always been particularly proud of himself when he observed his teachers walking the halls and holding the purple cards as though they were memorizing his advice. He foolishly assumed that he had inspired his staff to accept his particular brand of communication.

He had no idea that the *How to Talk to Parents* card had been replaced with the new and revised *How to Talk to Parents Who Are Assholes,* or that his parent–teacher advice card now looked like this:

Don't Say This:	Say This:
Your daughter is a slut.	Susie is very sociable and rarely without lunch money.
Your son stinks.	Johnny's farts rank 7.0 on the rectum scale.
Your kid is a gang-banger.	Your kid is making great progress getting admitted to the state penitentiary.
Your son/daughter is lazy.	Your child will continue to draw welfare just like his parents and grandparents before him.
Your son/daughter cheats.	Mary has a future in larceny and perhaps embezzlement.

Sometimes there were more challenges surviving as a high school teacher arising from the administrators and the parents than the students. Humor was just one of the tools that had enabled Nelly and her hard-working colleagues to manage despite often overwhelming odds.

She grabbed the stack of index cards and placed them in her computer case. I think Ford is living in Florida now, she mused. Maybe I can track down his address and send him these modifications. She got some real pleasure thinking of how horrified he would be to see his treasured training materials so desecrated.

Chapter 17

Jordan

A couple weeks after the cold spell, Nelly remembered her resolve to get a decent coat for Jordan. She had a few coupons to Kohl's and managed to buy a lined North face jacket for less than $20. She did not want Jordan to think of himself as a charity case, so she hired him to paint the study alcove in the back of her classroom. As he worked, he hummed softly.

Nelly was used to long stretches of silence around Jordan, but on this day, she sensed that something was troubling him. After observing him start to speak, then retreat, she asked him to take a break and drink a Coke with her. She pulled a couple drinks out of the mini-fridge, then handed one over.

"I need to tell you something, Ms. Nelson. I could be wrong, but I think Tonya Bishop is in trouble. I don't really talk to her that much, but she sits by me in American Literature. Lately she has been writing some weird stuff in her journal and she showed me a couple pages. At first I just thought it was some made-up story, but now I am not so sure. She said that her boyfriend is in some kind of danger and that he needs to get out of Colorado and that she is going with him. The thing is, I don't think she has ever met him in person."

Nelly thought about what she knew about Tonya. She was pleasant enough, but not the kind of student who stood out in any significant way. She had a couple of older siblings who were academic all-stars and athletes, and a dad who owned an impressive and highly profitable construction company. Nelly remembered how her parents had spent the entire parent-teacher conference discussing their older son and daughter. Whenever Nelly tried to bring the conversation around to Tonya, they admitted that she just did not measure up to the Bishop family standards. Her SAT scores were average, her grade point mediocre, and her school involvement minimal.

"Tell me more, Jordan. What worries you?"

"She has been corresponding with this guy she met on the internet, and she told me his name, so I checked it out online. If the guy I found is the same one, I am pretty sure that he's bad news. Anyway, she told me today that she was gonna leave Greeley for good. She said that she was leaving with this guy right after our class tomorrow but not to tell anyone. She wants her parents to think it is just a regular school day, and she figures they can get a big head start before anyone notices she is gone. I can't get involved, so I thought maybe you could do something."

Nelly thought about what she had just been told. It could be nothing, but Jordan had uncanny powers of observation, and she guessed that with his background that his instincts were likely correct. A girl like Tonya could easily be vulnerable; her siblings garnered the lion's share of the family's attention, and she had few, if any, friends. Like Jordan, she just blended in with the crowd, and remained largely invisible in mainstream high school. In fact, Nelly had assigned Jordan as her partner because she knew the two of them preferred to work alone, and neither one would intrude too much upon the other.

"Are you sure she's going to class tomorrow?"

"Yeah. She said that your class was the only one she cared about, and she didn't want to screw me over on the partner presentation tomorrow. She mentioned that her paycheck from Best Buy would not be ready until noon, and that she wanted to pick it up before she left town."

"OK. It may be nothing, Jordan, but let's figure this out. If I call her parents, they will want to know how I got this information, and I would have to tell them. Show me what you think you know about this guy."

Jordan switched seats with Nelly, then a few computer key strokes later, up came a news story about a 34-year-old local man, Jim Lorry, who had violated his parole and was now on the Weld County's *Most Wanted* list. He had burglarized several businesses, and a search warrant had unearthed an extensive porn collection. The picture was grainy, but recent, and Jordan committed it to memory. The article included a description of the vehicle he had stolen, his own grandmother's late model green Ford Taurus.

Nelly had become engaged in dozens of dramas over the years, but there was a fine line about when a teacher should become involved. There was always the chance that this was just another teenage girl's fabrication or wishful thinking. To notify parents over a possibility would be sheer foolishness. Besides, the guy in the paper was 34. Surely Tonya would not hook up with someone that much older. The Lorry name was relatively common in the area, too, so even if Jordan had the correct last name, it could be a different Lorry. Nelly frowned, mentally running through a whole series of possibilities.

"Would you just call her and get some more information?"

"I can't, Ms. Nelson. The only reason she said anything to me is because we were stuck as partners, and she needed me to cover for her while she texted the guy during class. It is not like we are real friends or anything. Besides, if the police ever get involved, I can't have them investigating me or my mother. You have to help; you just have to."

Something in his earnest expression convinced Nelly that she had no choice except to get involved. Although she harbored doubts about the whole situation, she still had the nagging intuition that this could be the real deal.

"OK, Jordan, this is what we are going to do. I will have you and Tonya give your report first. When you are finished, I will send you on an errand with the hall pass. Go outside and look around the visitors' parking lot. Since it is just outside my classroom, and the only accessible lot to the public, chances are this is where he will pick Tonya up. If you spot him, come back immediately. If you hand me the pass, I will know that it's time to get the police involved. I will have my phone and I can get the school resource officer out there right away. If you do not find him, I will confront Tonya myself; let me worry about what I will say. But I will not let her leave campus without the truth. This way I can keep your name out of it, but I could never live with myself if I let something bad happen. Either way, we will help her."

Jordan shifted uneasily in the seat, then thanked Nelly. He got up to finish the painting project, and once he finished, Nelly pulled out the North face jacket. She explained that it was payment for the work he had done. Jordan felt the warm lining of the jacket, broke into a huge smile, and thanked her once again. "I never had a new coat before, let alone a North face one. Normally I just wear Walmart stuff, but this is awesome!" He stuffed his threadbare old

Empty Desk

jacket into his backpack, gave Nelly a salute, and left the building for the day with a smile and a spring in his step.

Nelly slept fitfully that night, concerned about these two students in particular: one living a lie and the other perhaps about to do the same. That Jordan had cared enough for his classmate to tell Nelly revealed his good heart. The kid had every reason to be cynical and self-centered, but he was neither.

When she left for work the next morning, she mentally rehearsed several possible scenarios for the morning. None of them allayed her fears.

The first block of the school day took an eternity, so by the time American Literature rolled around, Nelly was a nervous wreck. As the students filed in, she glimpsed Jordan wearing his new jacket. He glanced furtively at her but said nothing. For several minutes after the tardy bell, there was no sign of Tonya, and Nelly's fear escalated. Just then the announcements started, and Tonya rushed in with a bulging backpack and a heavy purse. Nelly told her that since she arrived late she needed to stay a few minutes after class. Tonya mumbled an "OK."

After a number of meaningless announcements, Nelly indicated that the author projects would be first on the agenda. She reminded the class that each presentation would have a ten-minute time limit and that Tonya and Jordan would be first. Jordan reacted predictably. Never one to raise his hand or volunteer, he rose rather reluctantly to head to the front of the room. Tonya followed and proceeded to set up the poster they had worked on. An impressive ten minutes later, the two presenters handled a few audience questions, then returned to their desks.

Empty Desk

Nelly gave some feedback on the report, then handed Jordan a hall pass, requesting that he go to the print shop to pick up some handouts. Nelly selected the next group, who admitted that they were not prepared, so she continued down the list.

Tonya felt for her backpack, satisfied that it was still there. Nelly watched her pull a flip phone out of her pocket, type a few words, then hide it. Soon after, she started glancing out the window, but from her desk there was no clear view of the parking lot. By this time, Nelly was convinced that Jordan's intuition was spot on. She willed herself to calm down, then told the class to take a short in-room break, that she needed to check if her handouts were ready from the print shop.

She headed to the exit door, then spotted a green Taurus almost immediately. It was running and there was a male driver with a ball cap pulled over his face inside. Jordan was nowhere to be seen, so Nelly called Biggs, the school's resource officer and told him that she had spotted a green Taurus in the parking lot with a suspicious looking guy in it. Wasn't there a report in the news about a stolen Taurus? Could he check it out right away? Nelly counted on the fact that Biggs was the ultimate professional. She knew he carried a gun and was an excellent marksman, but the other two campus security guards had only Mace and a Taser for defense. Biggs had been a Marine and was trained to respond quickly, so from his vantage point in the security tower, he immediately spotted the vehicle. He told Nelly that he would radio the main office and that the school would go into temporary lockdown if there was a problem, so she should just "hold tight." Nelly breathed a sigh of relief that he had not asked too many questions.

Not wanting to alarm her students, Nelly slipped back into the classroom and called on the next group to present. She worried that Jordan might be in harm's way, but there was nothing she could do about it now. While Tonya wiggled in her desk and glanced repeatedly at the clock, Nelly continued with class. About ten minutes before the final bell, the athletic director made the all-school announcement that they were going to suspend the bells to test the security alarm. Teachers were to hold their classes until further notice. Tonya looked ready to freak out, but since students were not allowed to leave, she resigned herself to stay put.

What transpired next in the parking lot was an incredible series of lucky coincidences. Biggs sauntered over to the area, stopping to tell another driver that she needed to move along. As he chatted with the woman, he glanced at the license plate on the Taurus and confirmed that it matched that of the stolen vehicle. After she sped off, Lorry relaxed a little. This was just some stupid renta-cop, and he probably was going to make him move. Biggs greeted him amiably, told him about the rules for picking up students, and then asked him if he was aware of all the graffiti on his car. In fact, there was none, but the ruse worked to get Lorry to exit the vehicle. As soon as he got out of the car, Biggs grabbed him and forced his arm to his back.

By this time another school security officer Max Turner, completely unaware of the impending crisis, showed up to lend a hand. He was a cocky young guy completely full of himself and unnecessarily confident of his crime-fighting abilities.

"What's the problem?" he asked.

Empty Desk

Biggs kept Lorry pinned against the car and ordered Turner to get out his handcuffs. Ironically, Turner had forgotten to attach the cuffs to his own belt that morning, so he had to try to get the ones from Biggs. In the process, Lorry broke free and with Biggs and Turner in close pursuit, they raced toward the exit. Before they reached the exit, the gate unexpectedly and suddenly slammed shut with an incredible thud, trapping Lorry as the two guards wrestled him to the ground. Satisfied that he was under control, Biggs called 911. Within minutes, the Greeley police showed up, sirens blaring. They found no weapons on Lorry himself, and while one officer pushed him into the back seat of a squad car, another inspected the green Taurus.

In the commotion, which by this time had attracted the attention of some of the students who were ditching class or taking a smoke break, no one noticed the teenager in blue jeans with a North face jacket stroll away from the scene. Jordan Michaels had developed the uncanny ability to simply fade away when the circumstance required it. In his left hand he clutched a remote control for the parking lot gate, a device he had fashioned some time ago, never dreaming he might have a use for it so soon.

Nelly had no idea that Jordan had stealthily returned to campus the previous evening to tinker with the gate. Perhaps it was partly due to the legacy of his survivalist grandfather or the advice of the middle school janitor in Ohio or maybe even the skill set of his current shop teacher, but Jordan's expertise with all things mechanical enabled him to get in or exit anything. In his very first week at Horace Greeley High School, he had started planning for the possibility that he himself might have to flee. If he were ever being chased, it would be advantageous to delay the pursuer. You never know when the keys to a school or the control of a gate might work in your favor.

The crisis was handled as expertly as possible, and once the cops gave the all-clear, students left for their late lunches and the rumors started swirling. Biggs reported back to Ms. Nelson that Lorry was in jail and that the police had confiscated his cell phone. He admitted that there was a connection to someone in the school, but that he was not at liberty to tell her much more. He said that the whole operation worked like clockwork, but he was puzzled by the sudden shutting of the gate. Each morning he unlocked a heavy chain and manually rolled the gate to open the lot. The electrical part of it had not worked in years. "Must be my good karma," he joked.

The local news channel revealed the multiple charges that Lorry faced and the fact that two Horace Greeley security guards would share in the reward money. Nelly fumed when she heard that. The money was rightfully Jordan's, but she knew he would never want the publicity that went with it. She suspected that Jordan had had something to do with the gate, but they never spoke of the matter again. Just another secret of the hundreds a teacher keeps, thought Nelly.

Tonya Bishop never returned to Horace Greeley High School; her parents enrolled her in one of the new charter schools, and the administration never revealed her connection to Lorry. They had no idea that Jordan Michaels had most likely saved their daughter's life.

Chapter 18

Nelly

Nelly got up from her desk, stretched for a few moments, and then glanced out the window before resuming her desk excavation. The next item she found was Mary Smith's college essay. Mary Smith had graduated nearly twenty years prior, but Nelly could still picture her lovely blond hair, blue eyes, and charming smile. Mary's one outstanding feature was her absolute normalcy. In the tumultuous world of high school, there were many times when Nelly longed for a day without drama, fear, or regret. Sometimes it was refreshing to work with a student whose only pressing need was assistance with eliminating a comma splice. Mary, with her ordinary name, pleasant demeanor, nice family, and uncomplicated life was just such a person.

Nelly recalled, however, how frustrated Mary had been when the time came to select a subject for her college essay. At the time, Mary was almost jealous of her classmates whose lives had generated powerful stories, like how their youthful parents had neglected them, or how an emergency liver transplant saved their lives, or even how they escaped torture in their native countries before settling in the United States. How could she possibly compete with that?

Mary was absolutely certain that she had nothing notable about which to write. She took to heart the importance of making a strong first impression on admission officers, and she felt she was defeated before she even started on this essay. She struggled with generating a single sentence;

the mere thought of generating 500 words was like running a marathon in flip-flops.

"What am I gonna do, Ms. Nelson? I have nothing, absolutely nothing," she insisted.

Nelly ran through her standard list of suggestions, but nothing connected with the distraught senior.

"Everyone has a story, Mary. Go home and think about what makes you unique. Then just tell the truth. The story will resonate. I am sure of it."

"But Ms. Nelson, I have never traveled much. I don't know how to save anyone's life. I never made the winning goal. I am totally boring. What if no school wants me?"

"You are a special young lady. A college would be foolish not to admit you. Don't panic. It will come to you, I promise."

Mary left with a look of frustration bordering on despair, but she returned the following day with the first version of her essay, which Nelly now held in her hands. Nelly smiled broadly, remembering the first time she had read it. She scanned the opening lines of Mary Smith's essay.

I know my college essay is supposed to be some insightful masterpiece on some aspect of my life. I know it is supposed to be something that sets me apart from other applicants. It is supposed to make you pick me over another worthy candidate. The reality, though, is that I have not gone through chemotherapy, survived for months in a homeless shelter, or won a national robotics competition. As much as I don't want to reveal the truth about me, here it is:

My life is boring. I have a boring mother who stays at home except when we need her at a volleyball game or a PTA meeting. She makes great chocolate chip cookies, and usually has a hot meal on the table when my boring dad, an insurance salesman, gets home at precisely 6. Dad removes his tie and shoes as soon as he opens the door, then declares, "I'm home and hungry" to no one in particular. I have an uninteresting 14-year-old brother named John who plays-- of course--baseball. We live in the suburbs in a house with a white picket fence, a two-car garage, and a standard-sized backyard. There we play fetch with our dog, a lab, named--you won't believe this--Spot!

Every Sunday we all go to church together at 10:00 and sit with my grandparents. When get home, we always have a meal consisting of baked chicken and mashed potatoes, followed by apple pie with a single scoop of vanilla ice cream for dessert. Everything about my life is dull and predicable. My uncle even yawned at his own wedding, and it took a couple hours before anyone even noticed that my grandpa had died in his rocking chair.......

The essay proceeded from there with a plea for a chance to add to her experiences. It was filled with humor and warmth; apparently it had impressed several colleges, because Mary had been able to take her pick. She even secured a generous scholarship from her first choice: the University of Virginia.

Nelly placed the essay with the other *keepable* items. Her thoughts wandered back to Jordan Michaels. What if Jordan had had Mary's home and parents? What if he had been able to live a normal life in an ordinary neighborhood with a pet Labrador retriever and a room of his own? What then?

Chapter 19

Jordan

By the time Jordan reached his junior year, he was eager to earn his own money and to save some funds for college. So far, his forged identity had not generated any issues, and he decided that now was the time to test the waters. He had a real social security number, and his mother assured him that her "contacts" had legitimized his name change.

The truth was that high school was easy for him, and with limited social interaction, he had plenty of time to study and complete his assignments. His mother Judith had managed a consistent stretch of employment since moving to Colorado, but Jordan knew that it would not take long for her minimum wage paychecks and the leftover stolen drug money from their time in Ohio to disappear.

He rejected the typical teenagers' jobs. At places like McDonald's, the mall or the city swimming pool, he would inevitably run into his classmates. He did not want to explain his old life or risk saying something that might jeopardize his current living conditions. He decided that working at a nursing home would be a perfect fit. First, the work would likely be solitary and menial, and no high school kid he knew would even consider working around a bunch of old people. Gracious Manor Nursing Home was hiring, and since it was in walking distance from their apartment, he applied.

At the interview, he provided carefully rehearsed responses about his made-up life in Michigan and prayed that his potential employer Ken Mortensen knew little about the Saginaw-Bay City area. Fortunately, the manager was a Californian, and the only fact he knew about the state is that the Detroit Lions had a crappy football team. Although Mortensen hesitated to hire a teenager, he was a pretty good judge of character, and he thought Jordan looked like a good bet. Besides, it was not like he had a stack of applicants anyway.

They discussed his potential hours, and Jordan assured him that a shift or two during the week would be no problem during the school year. Besides, there would be weeks like spring break, summer vacation, and Christmas when he would not be in school at all. Jordan revealed that he was saving for college, the perfect declaration to convince his new employer that this kid would work out just fine.

Most workers at Gracious Manor never intended to make their employment there into a career; it was the sort of place one used to get some experience before advancing to a "real job." Plus, the work was often nasty. The sounds and smells were not for the faint of heart, and the turnover rate among staff and clientele was constant. It was, however, the perfect match for Jordan Michaels, and in a short period of time, the staff came to depend on him to do some of the more objectionable tasks.

Initially, his responsibilities were to clean and sanitize the rooms, hallways, public areas, and dining hall. He had special directions to follow to maintain the state's Health Department standards. He was to empty trash, attend to the two resident therapy dogs Barney and Fife, and keep up the grounds surrounding the facility. Gradually, he would notice other maintenance items that needed attention, and to the delight of his employer, Jordan was able to fix most problems. Later, Jordan became the go-to guy for leaky toilets, loose fixtures, noisy fans, and squeaky beds.

Before long, the caregivers began to trust Jordan to transport the residents to the dining hall, where they were generally assigned tables according to their room numbers. This arrangement enabled the servers to identify those who required special diets more easily. However, the residents, many of whom had survived a couple world wars, were no pushovers. They had their personal preferences about where and with whom they wished to share a meal, and Jordan did his best to accommodate those wishes.

One resident named Sophia talked non-stop about anything and everything; she had been at Gracious Manor for over eight years and served as the unofficial tattletale. "Margaret soiled the sheets again," she declared to anyone who was listening. "She should get a write-up on that one. And Jonas is eating too much. He had four pieces of cheesecake already today." This diatribe went on constantly; most people ignored her, or they avoided her altogether. Even the hired help steered clear, since she was sure to report even the mildest slipup to Mr. Mortensen. Once she got a young kitchen worker fired for leaving the kitchen area to take personal phone calls. It was little wonder that no one wanted to sit with her, so Jordan did his best to rotate the people so that this burden could be distributed as equitably as possible.

Within just a few weeks, Jordan realized just how toxic Sophia could be. She taunted Elise, who suffered from Parkinson's, for her "terrible table manners." Under the guise of helping the partially blind Rob open his mail, Sophia would slip some of the cash his family sent into her own sweater pocket. She even stuck her foot out to trip Annie, who up until then had managed to avoid using a walker. Jordan's powers of observation were spot-on, and he could recognize a bully when he saw one. He realized that even in a nursing home, even when people are close to death, they can manage to sink to the depths of the human condition. He resolved to keep extra vigilant around Sophia and do his best to mitigate her damage. These fragile and vulnerable people deserved better.

Sophia had one of the better views from her room in the north wing. Her window overlooked a green space and featured a hummingbird feeder extended over the bough of a tree. She had the prime real estate for viewing and occasionally allowed others in her room to see the birds. Not much happened at Gracious Manor, so this was a big deal. She acted like a virtual mafia boss as she parceled out viewing times and opportunities in an inordinately stingy fashion.

Her large window, a rare feature in the facility, had moveable shutters that she could control from inside her suite. In a particularly mean-spirited move, she positioned the left shutter so that it obscured the bird-viewing of her closest neighbor, Harriet Goldstein. Harriet had survived the Holocaust in a concentration camp, and the only pleasure of her time there had been observing the birds flying freely over Sobibor. For some unknown reason, Sophia had never liked Jews, and she did little to disguise that fact. The shutter move was just one of a string of indignities that she imposed on the kind-hearted Harriet.

Since moving to Colorado, Jordan had made it a practice to stay out of people's business, but he couldn't help but think of how he would have wanted someone to care about Gramps. So, in honor of Gramps, Jordan resolved to do a little something to make Harriet smile. He had plenty of time while cleaning to think about the folks at Gracious Manor and what he might do to make their stay there a little more comfortable. After getting permission from Mr. Mortensen, Jordan got a couple of the old guys who lived there to help him build some state-of-the-art bird houses and bat houses for use on the grounds. Neither had held hammers and screwdrivers for years, and they were pleased to be asked for their expertise. They engaged in the project with unbridled enthusiasm, laughing at their mistakes and sharing exaggerated stories of their former glory as contractors and electricians. Several of the women residents still loved to paint and do other crafts so they happily put charming finishing touches on the projects.

Mr. Mortensen could not have been more pleased about the whole project. Not only had it given a few residents something to do, but it would be a source of entertainment for many for years to come. Mortensen mentally congratulated himself for his wisdom in hiring Jordan. He had already consulted his buddy who worked for the forest service about where to locate the bat houses, but he decided to let Jordan determine the location of the bird houses.

This decision was an easy one for Jordan. He stopped by Harriet's room to ask her which of the birdhouses she would like to have placed outside her window. Harriet eyes welled up with tears as she weighed her options. "Really? I get to pick?" she queried. Jordan smiled and nodded. Sophia overheard the conversation and stepped out into the hallway to tell Jordan that since she had been there longer than Harriet, she should be the one to

Empty Desk

determine bird house placement. In the politest tone he could manage, he let Sophia know that she already had the hummingbirds, and it was someone else's turn.

As Jordan set about installing the first bird house on a pole outside of Harriet's window, he took care to place it just outside of the sight of Sophia. In fact, in a subversive move of his own, he reached over to Sophia's window shutter and placed a small bracket on the base of it to prevent the shutter from ever fully closing. The result was that Sophia would never see the spectacular performance and jubilant concert that the plum-colored starlings and paradise fly-catchers would put on.

Within days, Harriet's room became the social center for the north wing as she welcomed her neighbors in for tea and viewings. Some of the computer savvy residents started studying the habits of their feathered friends and before long the perfect seeds and suet drew a daily kaleidoscope of subjects.

Just about everyone was fully aware that Sophia now sat alone in her suite, no longer the queen bee of the aviary world. Most of them smiled about it, and a few even snickered openly. Jordan now understood what Gramps meant years ago when he had assured him, "What goes around comes around." Indeed!

Chapter 20

Nelly

Nelly felt along the base of the secret drawer and located a thin silver cross on a narrow chain. It had been a parting gift from Tabitha Russell, a gentle and gracious young lady whose story Nelly feared would have a disastrous ending. Nelly wondered if she had done the right thing when she reported her suspicions about Tabitha's home life to the county's Department of Health and Social Services.

Tabitha was one of seven children of Lisa and Joseph Russell. They were a well-known and well-respected Morman family, with Joseph serving a significant amount of time as the precinct's bishop. Each Russell child was a teacher's dream. Their work, without exception, was on time, articulate, insightful, and almost always perfect. Despite what Nelly assumed was a strict and conservative background, Tabitha studied controversial texts like *Catcher in the Rye, Color Purple,* and *Handmaid's Tale* with an open mind and keen insight. The high school had a fairly large Morman population, and Nelly had come to appreciate how much her Morman students relished great literature, regardless of its often sensitive and controversial nature.

Over the years, Nelly occasionally had to handle objections of evangelical Christian parents to the titles assigned in the Advanced Placement English curriculum. Like most English teachers, she had endured her fair share of criticism for being too liberal, or for promoting the repugnant "public school" agenda. When asked, she usually would substitute a replacement title for one of the required novels if the parents requested one; if they wanted further exceptions, Nelly would refuse and recommend the students take an alternate course. Most of the time, the students wanted the course (and Ms. Nelson as the teacher), so the matter could be quickly resolved.

Ms. Nelson had a standard speech to parents that normally quieted their fears. "Dealing with controversy and analyzing social and historical issues in literature is an important skill," she would say. "In this class, I concentrate on developing critical thinking. Here all viewpoints can be expressed and respected. I encourage you as parents to read and discuss the novels with your children. You are invited to join us for our in-class discussions." Since most of the parents did not have the time nor the desire to do that, and their children would be mortified to have a mom or dad come to class with them, the challenges were usually short-lived.

Occasionally, some religious zealot would threaten to take the matter to the school board, but Nelly had the experience and generally the expertise to assure parents that the approved literature would hardly corrupt their offspring. Few parents wanted to admit that reading *Death of a Salesman* would turn their kid into an adulterer or that Holden Caulfield's use of an expletive would make them delinquents, so most were content to make strong objections and let the matter go. Putting up with parental bullying was just part of the job, and Nelly had learned how to diffuse it. The Russell parents had not been pleased with *Ethan Frome* as required reading, but refrained from making any serious objections, deciding instead "to trust Tabitha's moral fiber."

Empty Desk

Tabitha was a quiet and puzzling young lady. Her auburn hair extended well beyond her waist, but she rarely wore it loose. Instead she braided it tightly and cinched it with a sturdy rubber band and a single white ribbon. Nelly had never seen her wear makeup, jewelry, or even blue jeans. Most often her attire consisted of a maxi-length denim dress that fully covered her arms and legs.

Her fellow students had never spotted her at a football game or student council meeting and just assumed that her parents were strict. Like Jordan, she managed to keep to herself except for the required group projects. Her scores on tests and projects consistently outpaced those of her classmates. Since she was so quiet, the class always seemed surprised when she did speak up. They were even more surprised when her viewpoints did not conform to their stereotypes of religious types. Once she gave a particularly persuasive speech about advancing women's rights for equal pay and decent health care. In the question-and-answer session afterwards, another student asked about whether her own religion oppressed women. She stammered, "No," before moving quickly to the next question. Tabitha remained flustered for the rest of the class period, and Nelly suspected that the question had struck one very vulnerable nerve.

Nelly's first clue that something might be amiss in the Russell household came when Tabitha expressed a surprisingly empathetic view of Hester Prynne's daughter Pearl from the *Scarlet Letter*. Her comments in the class discussion and later in the analytical paper were far from the norm. Something told Nelly that she spoke more from experience than *Cliff Notes*.

One afternoon the class had a spirited conversation about mothers. The topic arose over a discussion of Cathy

Ames, the moral monster in the novel *East of Eden*, who abandons her twin sons. Students shared their perceptions of the role that mothers played in their own lives. Some told stories of helicopter mothers who hovered over them constantly; others revealed that they barely knew their mothers. One student admitted that her mother was in jail. Tabitha's only comment was that people have no idea what a mother is really like behind closed doors, and they should not assume that a typical family with a mom and dad in the household is any better than another kind of home.

Nelly's nagging concern was later reinforced with Tabitha's research paper on the prophet Warren Jeffs and his legal battles regarding the polygamous compound in Colorado City, Arizona. The detailed, well-documented, and clearly organized paper expressed not only allegiance to prophets like Jeffs but also an uneasiness about polygamy.

The day she returned the papers to the class, Nellie gave the students a reading assignment, then called each one up individually to see if they had any questions about their papers. She liked these one-on-one sessions because they helped both teacher and student to understand what needed to be done to prepare for college-level writing. Most had performed well on the project, and Nelly enjoyed the opportunity to lavish praise on kids or to assure others that their writing flaws were easily fixable.

Her meeting with Tabitha started with an easy conversation about all the strengths in the paper, and Tabitha was clearly pleased with the feedback. When Nelly got around to the thesis of the paper, she inquired about Tabitha's position on the topic of polygamy and suggested that she state it more clearly.

"I can't do that. My pastor speaks for me on all matters of the church. I must follow his vision or risk having my recommend revoked. My pastor has continuing revelations, and my family is divinely anointed. Besides, perfect obedience produces perfect faith."

Nelly let this comment sink in, struck by the rather rehearsed tone of the response. She pondered her own sparse knowledge of the Morman religion. She remembered reading about the "recommend" in the Morman church, and vaguely recalled the role of revelations to the followers. She knew that polygamy was not a tenet of the modern Morman church, but that it still was practiced in breakaway fundamentalist sects.

She chose not to pursue the matter further, and instead commented on how well Tabitha's cousin Brenda had adjusted to Horace Greeley High School and how wonderful it was that the Russells had taken in two of their relatives. The story Nelly had been told was that Brenda and her sister Susan, cousins of Tabitha, had come to stay with the Russell family after the tragic death of their parents.

Tabitha immediately bristled at the mention of Brenda, and Nelly realized that she had brought up a sore spot. Not wanting to upset her, Nelly reached for Tabitha's hand and assured her that adjusting to changes in the family structure is tough for everyone. If any family could make the situation work, it would be the Russells. Tabitha burst into tears, and before long was a heaving bundle of convulsions. Nelly slipped her the hall pass, and she stayed out of the room until the passing period. When she returned, she was fully composed, but Nelly checked to make sure that she was okay.

"What is the matter, Tabitha? Is there anything I can do to help?"

"It is not what you think, Ms. Nelson. Brenda....Mom.....I just can't talk about it. I'm sorry for crying like this, and I will just need to pray about the changes in my life. I must do God's bidding and follow the teachings of my church."

"Of course, dear. I do not mean to pry, but if you need to talk to someone, I can refer you to a counselor. Anything you say would be confidential, and sometimes it helps to get concerns out in the open."

"I could never do that. My father would be so disappointed. So would my mothers. Mother."

Nelly caught the plural *mothers*, and instinctively considered whether her cousin Brenda might be a second or third wife of Mr. Russell. Surely not. Yet Tabitha's actions and words over the course of the semester indicated that that something was obviously troubling her, and this explanation fit. Nelly shook off the preposterous idea, but an interaction she observed between Brenda and Tabitha a few days later only affirmed her initial speculations.

Brenda approached Tabitha in the hallway and pulled her aside with a rather fierce scolding about not finishing her chores that morning. She berated her for past offences like not pulling the weeds in front of the house and forgetting to water the plants. The whole scene baffled Nelly. It was not a cousin-to-cousin discussion, but much more like one between a parent and her child. Nelly made a mental note to keep an eye on the situation.

Over the following few weeks, Tabitha withdrew further and further into herself, and her perfect attendance record became marred with routine absences. Nelly noticed that her complexion had become very pale and she continued to lose weight. She took to biting her fingernails until there was nothing left and frequently asked for the hall pass.

Out of concern for Tabitha, Nelly followed her to the restroom one day, and listened as the girl vomited in the stall. Nelly waited for her to finish, then insisted that she go to the school nurse. Unfortunately, the nurse was out of the office for the day. While there, though, Tabitha broke down again, this time admitting that she could not bear to live anymore. Nelly told Tabitha that she would call her parents and wait with her until they came to get her.

When Lisa Russell arrived to pick up her daughter, Nelly spoke frankly to her about her growing concern about Tabitha's physical and mental health. Mrs. Russell thanked her but assured her that there was nothing to worry about. After that day, Tabitha returned to school only once. She came to clean out her locker and to give Nelly the tiny cross that she now held in her hands.

"I am going to be homeschooled from now on. My family will be moving back to Utah this summer, and God has special plans for me there. I want to thank you for helping me. I will be just fine."

Nelly hugged Tabitha and wished her well. The girl held onto Nelly tightly, then smiled through tears. The word *Help* came out in a tiny whisper before she fled from the room.

That single syllable haunted Nelly the entire day. Not knowing what else to do, Nelly headed to the office of Child and Family Services after work and laid out her suspicions. It was a delicate situation, and the last thing Nelly wanted was to disrupt a decent family's life. She was grateful that the identities of teachers who report suspected abuse are protected, and relieved when the agent assured her that the matter would be handled professionally.

She never heard from Tabitha or Child & Family Services again, but the Russells put the family's home up for sale the following week. She heard that they moved back to Utah. Nelly grasped the tiny cross, kissed it with a fervent wish that Tabitha was living the life she truly wanted, and placed it with the other items in her duffel bag.

Chapter 21

Jordan

At the start of Jordan's junior year, he stopped by after school one afternoon to fill Nelly in on his summer activities. He was relieved to see his favorite teacher after the long summer, and he wanted to tell her about his job. He still wore the same plain tee-shirts and blue jeans, still exuded very little expression, still sort of receded into the background. But he had filled out and his skin had been bronzed by the Colorado sun. His acne had almost disappeared, and his blue eyes carried an intensity she had not noticed previously. He was becoming a man, and a sturdy one at that.

Nelly had learned of his near perfect PSAT score at the end of his sophomore year, and she was excited to keep him going on a rigorous academic tract for the college-bound. By now, she knew that even if he might secretly want recognition, friends, or typical teenage experiences that he would not seek them out. He would, however, keep learning and pursuing his dream of a college education. He had never fully abandoned his former life as David Martin, and Nelly was quite sure that he never would. Until he completed high school, he was forever looking over his shoulder, wondering if his past would catch up with him.

"How are you, Jordan? Did you have a good summer?"

"I am okay. Summer was okay, too. My mom is having a hard time, but I have a job and it is enough to help get the bills paid."

Nelly did not want to pry too much, but she sensed that Jordan needed to talk. She had always resented when her colleagues asked too many questions about her own summers, so she decided to let Jordan take the lead in the conversation.

She had thought about Jordan over the break, particularly when her summer assignment required her to solve several identity theft cases. At the time, she considered her own vulnerability due to harboring Jordan's secrets. The public rarely understood the fine line that teachers walked between keeping a student's confidence and legally being required to contact authorities about potential danger to them. Nelly suspected that she already knew too much about the teenager in front of her and hoped that he would be smart about how much he revealed.

Jordan glanced around the classroom, and immediately noticed that the flag stand was hanging off the wall haphazardly and the pencil sharpener had been placed on a desk near where it had fallen from the wall. "Looks like you can still use a hand, Ms. Nelson," he joked, "Good thing I came prepared." He reached into the backpack and selected a couple of tools. As he made the minor repairs, he chatted about his activities over the previous weeks.

"I got a job at Gracious Manor this summer, and they are going to keep me on for the school year. I started working in the kitchen and bringing meals to the rooms of the old people who couldn't make it to the cafeteria. I guess they must really need help with the people in the dementia wing, so they transferred me over there to help with cleaning and maintenance in that area."

Empty Desk

Nelly thought about how difficult that job could be. She understood, though, that Jordan probably picked it to stay out of the limelight. A job with other teenagers would mean making friends and sharing his personal life; Gracious Manor would be the perfect place to simply do the job and then head home. Nelly's neighbor, now a retired nurse, had worked there previously, and often commented on the lousy work environment and constant turnover.

"Do you like working there?" Ms. Nelson inquired.

"I do. I mean, the people there are suffering, but they always are glad to see me. I don't get grossed out too easily—my grandpa taught me that—and I get to work the hours I want. Some of those people never get a visitor and they like me. The stuff I have to fix is not very hard, and most of the residents are grateful for someone to clean up their rooms. They all have stories to share, and you taught me to appreciate stories, so I listen to them. I even got to help some of the residents build birdhouses, and that was a lot of fun."

Jordan smiled, "There is one old guy, Mr. Stevens, who reminds me of my grandpa. I don't think he has any family, so I talk to him a lot. It is a little weird because I need to re-introduce myself to him every day because his mind is going, but he's a cool guy. I don't have to be on my guard around him either because he forgets things as soon as I tell him. I like having somebody to talk to, though."

Nelly contemplated how unusual it was for a 17-year-old to embrace grunt work, old people, and low pay. She could not think of another student who would describe building birdhouses with the elderly as fun. It was just another reason that Jordan would forever remain one of her all-time favorite people, and she mentally affirmed her resolve to do what she could to help him for as long as she could. For a moment, she regretted not having children of her own.

"You mentioned your mom was having a hard time. That must be tough for you too." Nelly deliberately refrained from asking a question. It was best, she decided, to let Jordan share what he wanted.

Jordan now stood at her desk. As he unzipped the backpack to tuck away his tools, she noticed his chin quivered and he started blinking away what were likely tears.

"I think she might be dealing drugs again. I don't know what is happening with Walmart. She says that there is nothing wrong, but I know better. She tells me that I shouldn't worry, but I do. I told her if money is a problem that I would work the whole night shift and go to school days, but she doesn't want that. I think there is more going on, though, cuz she looks tired all the time and sometimes she does not come home."

Nelly did not know what to say, so she remained silent. She turned to academics and tried to focus Jordan's attention on the upcoming school year. She congratulated him on the great test scores and assured him that with those and his solid grade point average that he could earn plenty of college scholarships. It seemed to brighten his mood. They went over his schedule, and Nelly was pleased to see that he had enrolled in Mr. Diaz's Advanced Placement Chemistry course. Diaz was a brilliant scientist and an even better teacher, just the sort of mentor that Jordan needed.

"I have to take off now, Ms. Nelson. I will see you Monday in A.P. English class. I already read the books for the semester, too."

"That does not surprise me, Jordan, I look forward to hearing what you think about *Candide*. Take care. See you soon."

Nelly dropped a pen and bent to pick it up. Just like that, Jordan was gone.

Chapter 22

Nelly

Nelly shoved a few more trinkets into her duffel bag with the thought she would sort through them more carefully once she got home. A postcard with a beautifully sketched gecko fell to the floor. The memory associated with the sketch made Nelly laugh out loud. She recalled the assignment that led to one of her favorite stories from the many she gathered over her career.

As part of a lesson on using imagery, Nelly required students to describe an object that had great personal meaning to them. They had to explain how they acquired the object, why it was meaningful, and how its meaning evolved over time. Even though the students usually complained that there was nothing to write about, the truth is that each one had such an item.

Often it would be a piece of jewelry handed down from a grandparent, a trophy from middle school, or a favorite doll or toy. Some of the stories were heart-wrenching, like the one based on a note a dying mom had given her daughter or the dog tags that a fallen soldier from Desert Storm had left his son. Sometimes, though, the stories would capture the great joy of childhood, an incredible camping vacation, or some particularly charming holiday ritual in a family's history.

The card in her hand was dated April 3, 1995 and under the green and white drawing of the gecko Harley Minelli had scrawled his signature and a smiley face. Every year since that freshman writing class, Harley would send Nelly a Christmas card reminding her of the effects of that assignment. And every year Nelly would smile broadly as she recalled the event fondly.

Apparently, Harley's parents were opposed to pets—any pets. They had full-time jobs, a limited budget, and kids with severe allergies, so despite the pleas of their children, they said *No* to the constant requests for dogs or cats or birds. Harley felt deprived when he visited his friends' homes and every one of them had a canine companion or two. It was just not fair.

The summer before high school, Harley took on a part time job cleaning the local swimming pool. He barely made minimum wage and worked very few hours, but he knew immediately how he would spend his money. He would make his goal of having a pet of his own come true.

He started out with big dreams—a golden retriever at first, then a Siamese cat. His parents reaffirmed their objections, reminding him of all the family members with allergies. They warned him about the required shots and licensing, the cost of food, and the need for a plan for the animal when they were not home.

Reluctantly, Harley had to adjust his thinking. He eliminated a bird because they were messy and noisy. His mother absolutely refused to even consider a snake, and his dad was outraged at the mere mention of a pot-bellied pig. After consulting a few library books and finding a cheap cage at a garage sale, Harley settled on a gecko he had spotted at the local pet shop. Since he had spent his own money, and geckoes did not carry the built-in problems associated with most other creatures, the Minellis relented and grudgingly accepted the new family member to their ranks.

Harley named his acquisition Harley Jr. and the two creatures developed a great interactive relationship. Theirs was an easy friendship, and Harley found himself confiding in his namesake about his troubles as well as his lofty plans for the future. The gecko would stare intently, often raising his tiny head as if to affirm whatever Harley told him.

Harley built a comfortable miniature maze and gazebo within the cage and refreshed it with mulch often. At times, he would release the critter so that he could chase crickets or climb up celery stalks. When Harley would call to him, he would respond, racing over to crawl into Harley's outstretched hand. He was no guard dog or prize-winning feline, but to Harley he was a true friend.

Harley wrote a particularly captivating essay about his unusual pet, and Nelly encouraged him to bring Harley Jr. to class on "Share Day." Teenagers are chronic complainers, and this high school version of Show-and-Tell invariably generated a tsunami of objections. They found it juvenile and stupid, but by the time the classes ended, they were so enthralled by their classmates' stories that they begged to do it again.

Harley was so excited to show off his pet that he even gave him a bath the night before and arranged the inside of the cage as artistically as he could. He lectured Harley Jr. the night before about how he would be center stage the next day and he expected Harley Jr. to show off his best skills. No gold watch or heirloom wedding gown or autographed football would hold a candle to the pet Harley loved.

Harley did not want to lug the cage, his lunch, and a bulging backpack on the bus, so he talked his mother into driving him to school the next morning. Ann Minelli rearranged her work schedule so that she could run the cage back home after Harley's presentation before she reported to her job at the post office. She was secretly pleased that Harley was so enthused about a school assignment, and this fact put her in a particularly good mood.

Harley threw his lunch and backpack into the back seat of their 1990 Chevy Capri but carried the cage with him as he eased into the passenger side front seat. Ann hummed a verse of "Stop in the Name of Love" as they left the driveway and headed to the highway. Harley fingered the latch on the cage and coached the gecko out onto his hand. For several minutes, he talked to his little friend, and Ann could not help but smile. She realized that this moment would pass all too soon, and before she knew it Harley would be an adult. It was best to enjoy these waning moments of childhood, she thought.

The highway was particularly busy that morning, and they were in the height of rush hour. After cruising along at a brisk pace for several miles, the traffic flow came to a rather abrupt stop. When Ann hit the brakes, the tiny gecko flew out of Harley's hands, sailed across Ann's lap, and landed somewhere near the gas pedal.

The traffic started moving again, and Ann started screaming at both Harleys as she tried to maintain control of the steering wheel. The animal was terrified and darted around frantically before racing up her left leg and under her skirt. She had not worn panty hose that morning and Harley Jr.'s toe pads scurrying around her upper thighs freaked her out. When Harley saw the sheer panic in his mother, he had no thought except to save his delicate friend from what could clearly be death.

Empty Desk

"Stop. Pull over. Don't hurt him, Mom!" Harley screamed as his mother instinctively batted at the movement between her legs.

Ann Minelli turned on her blinker and pulled as far as she could to the side of the road. She yelled a few expletives at her son, opened the door as soon as it was safe, and headed to the green area where she frantically started jumping up and down to extricate the gecko from under her skirt.

Harley Jr. held on for dear life as Ann panicked, her screams echoing down the highway as commuters buzzed by on their way to work or school.

As luck would have it, a nursing student from the nearby community college noticed the struggling woman at the side of the road. His class had not yet studied the chapter on epilepsy, but he felt certain that he could accurately identify an epileptic seizure when he saw one. He swerved off the side of the road, grabbing his wallet to stick in the woman's mouth to prevent her from swallowing her tongue. Never mind that this was no seizure. Never mind that the woman was hysterically telling him NO. Never mind that people cannot swallow their tongues. The boy near the woman was gesturing wildly, yelling that someone was going to die, and those words convinced Norman Deyo that today he would save someone's life.

As Norman tried to force his germ-laden wallet into Ann's mouth, she continued jumping up and down holding her stomach muttering something indecipherable. The boy was beside himself with worry for his beloved gecko and when there was no stopping the well-meaning nursing student, Harley signaled a passing trucker for help. The trucker could not believe that some brazen jerk was attacking a woman in broad daylight, in front of a child for God's sake, but he knew exactly how to put a stop to the incident. He eased his truck to the side of the road, flew out of the vehicle, and without hesitation raced over to the struggling man and woman before landing a powerful punch to the offender's jaw.

The blow was enough to render Norman into a stunned fog, and the pause enabled Ann to reveal that she had a gecko stuck under her skirt. The trucker driver had no idea what a gecko was, but the word alone incensed him further. In a desperate attempt to save his precious pet, Harley grabbed the trucker's shirt and screamed, "Stop! Stop! It's my lizard, my lizard. We have to save him," The command halted the trucker's aggression just long enough for Norman to tell him about the seizure, and to restore a bit of sanity to the otherwise ridiculous chain of events.

Just then the wailing sirens of the Colorado State Patrol interrupted the frantic scenario. Two strapping officers emerged from the squad car with their hands on their weapons. By this time, Ann's hysteria was a convoluted combination of both laughter and tears; not knowing what else to do and convinced that she would be shot if she turned her back to the officers, she abandoned all modesty and raised her skirt. Hand shaking, she tenderly removed a tiny lizard-like creature that had curled into a fetal position from the outside of her white cotton granny panties.

As Harley reached for his namesake, the stunned animal scampered into Harley's outstretched hand. Not willing to risk another escape, Harley headed back to the car, where he placed the gecko safely in the cage and secured the latch. It took a full fifteen minutes to bring all the parties up to speed on what had happened. Norman rejected the offer to press charges against the trucker, and everyone shared a laugh over the entire affair.

Harley knew that he was already late for school, but he would get to Ms. Nelson's class on time. Knowing how much Ms. Nelson loved stories, Harley got an idea. What if he could talk everyone into coming to class with him? What if everyone told the story? It would be an epic presentation.

Despite busy schedules for all involved, the mother, the nursing student, the trucker, one of the state patrolmen, and the high school freshman managed to accompany a bedraggled gecko to Room 203 at Horace Greeley High School to tell a story.

And a good one it was.

Chapter 23

Jordan

Jordan enjoyed Mr. Diaz's A.P. Chemistry class so much that he started showing up a little early to help him stage his daily experiments. Diaz knew that his students, all what most high school students would call *geeks,* reveled in the somewhat nerdy demonstrations of explosions and chemical reactions. The students had come to expect something entertaining every day, and he rarely disappointed them.

The experiments started with simple demonstrations of density drinks and fizz inflators. Later the students constructed soap-powered model boats and levitating orbs. By the end of the semester, they understood the interactions of most chemical reactions and could calculate the math behind the power of everything from fireworks to bombs. The class was so rigorous that only a hearty dozen or so students managed to tough it out, and Diaz was proud of their dedication. He often reminded them of the responsibility that comes with understanding and applying chemistry to the real world and encouraged them to pursue careers in science.

One of the new students, Nick Samuels, transferred in at semester, and he immediately caught the attention of the class. He was an attractive young man with long curly red hair and a generous array of freckles. He stood an impressive 6' 3" and often wore expensive name-brand clothes and shoes. He hailed from a pricey West coast private school and lived in the lavish Keystone area south of town. He had an air of entitlement, but also a keen intellect, so this class was the perfect placement.

His parents came from money and neither worked, spending most of their time traveling extensively seeking unique art to add to their already impressive collection. Nick was often left with his "manny," a rather stately gentleman who saw to it that Nick had food, transportation, and at least a little supervision. Nick could have passed for a *Gentlemen's Quarterly* model, but the scowl on his face and glaring eyes put off distinct vibes to stay away.

So that's what everyone did. A few girls tried to flirt with him, but after a sneer and a cool rebuff, they left him alone. Something was a just little off with him. This perception heightened when the class first started to study bombs and chemical warfare. For the first time all semester, Nick paid close attention and asked questions. He started carting around books on the Manhattan Project and Agent Orange. He often had to be pulled off websites devoted to these subjects, and Diaz had commented a time or two on his unusual fascination with all things explosive.

Much to his delight, Nick won the class Bottle Rocket competition, and bragged to the class that he owned a virtual arsenal of both fireworks and firearms. Maybe it was Jordan's connection with the criminal element in his own past, but he began to worry about Nick's mental state. He had more than an inkling that Nick was either hiding something illegal or planning something dangerous.

Since most of his classmates naturally gravitated to their friends when required to partner up, Jordan ended up with Nick more often than not. The two of them preferred to keep to out of the mainstream, so the arrangement suited them both.

It was during this time that Jordan learned that Nick had been placed on probation for driving while his license had been suspended for a series of DUI's. Nick had a sleek new SUV of his own, but his parents had commandeered all the keys, an action that enraged Nick. Apparently, the move to Colorado had been precipitated by multiple poor choices, and his parents wanted him in a new environment with greater supervision than before. Besides, here they were within an hour's drive to their vacation home in Vail.

Nick was incredibly self-absorbed, and as the two of them worked on the assigned labs, he revealed more about himself. Most of those A.P. Chemistry experiments required a good deal of time and patience, so while waiting for results Nick would fill the time with a running commentary on the unfairness of adults and ridiculousness of the school. Sometimes he chatted about how fun it would be to blow things up. Jordan feigned being interested, asking a few questions here and there, but deliberately avoided reacting much to Nick's bragging. It never occurred to Nick to question Jordan about his background; in fact, he found his lab partner a real nothing. Jordan was a decent listener, though, and seemed in agreement about how lame the school and its teachers were, so the two continued to be lab partners.

Nick couldn't wait to finish the school year. He hated anyone remotely connected to law enforcement and bragged that they were nothing but stupid pigs. It was clear he had little use for his classmates, parents, or teachers. He was simply putting in his time until he could get back to California to resume whatever it was that he had been doing previously. He remarked that he had a court date coming up, and once that was over, he'd get

Empty Desk

his car back and would waste no time in getting out of Colorado. Jordan mostly nodded, only occasionally offering a response.

Ironically, it was Mr. Diaz's insistence on constant vigilance and keen observation when dealing with chemicals that first alerted Jordan to Nick's terror plot. Like Jordan, Nick had an unusual backpack and one day when he set it down, Jordan noticed that it contained a good-sized container of a popular pool cleaner. They had just learned in one of previous week's sessions that pool cleaner was a common ingredient in homemade improvised explosive devices. Jordan wondered if Nick planned on making an IED and decided to keep an eye on Nick in the days to come.

Within a week of spotting the pool cleaner, Jordan observed Nick messing around with some vials in the cupboards toward the back of the classroom. Diaz was wearing goggles and totally absorbed in helping another student, so he had no clue when Nick slipped something into his jacket pockets. Jordan noticed, though, and the alarm bells went off. Still painfully aware of the necessity of protecting his own secrets, Jordan simply watched and waited.

One particularly gloomy day, Nick arrived late to class with a nasty look on his face and a menacing swagger. Diaz glanced at the pass and noticed that he had been excused due to court. Judging from Nick's demeanor, it must not have gone well. Diaz thought better of quizzing him about it and decided to ignore his student as he growled and slammed himself into the chair where he remained for the full sixty minutes of class.

Empty Desk

Jordan speculated the reason for his anger was that maybe he was not off probation after all, and more likely than not, the sports car was still off limits.

The semester meandered on, and although Nick never missed class, he became increasingly fidgety and agitated. It was not uncommon for him to cuss loudly if he disliked a score on a quiz or to crumble up a handout and toss it across the room. Jordan's biological dad had had anger issues, and although he had not seen David Martin in years, observing Nick's nonverbal behavior brought back a slew of memories, none of them pleasant.

Something was going to happen; of this Jordan was certain. But what? Suicide? A bomb? Maybe knocking off his parents? Nick was hardly a friend, and Jordan had enough good sense to stay away from him, except for those lab days when they both needed a lab partner.

Jordan thought about talking to Ms. Nelson about it, but he really did not want her involved; she had already stuck her neck out helping Tonya Bishop, and that was enough. He already knew what his mother would say if he asked her. Besides, she had her own problems to deal with. Jordan decided to try to figure out a plan to sabotage whatever Nick had up his sleeve. For a moment, the image of Gramps appeared, and Jordan missed him so badly it hurt. What would he do? Gramps would outsmart him. So that's exactly what Jordan resolved to do.

One day the following week, Nick strolled into the class lit up like a Christmas tree. Gone was the scowl and the anger. Instead, he exuded euphoria.

"Hey, suckers!" he declared.

Empty Desk

"Who you calling a sucker?" yelled Shelly Hayes.

"All of you assholes. Today is gonna be your lucky day. You won't be forgetting this day…"

"Why? They gonna cancel school or something?"

"Yeah, something."

Just then Jordan spotted Nick's backpack, not his usual one, but a new one with layers of bubble wrap sticking out of the end of it. He had cared enough about something to wrap it up to protect it. Jordan noticed that Nick was not uncomfortable in the least about being close to the backpack, so he relaxed a little. Jordan figured that Nick was probably not someone who would off himself….too much of an ego. He probably wouldn't want to get in any more legal trouble, either, so if he really were up to something, chances are it was something that would not get traced back to him.

Jordan pulled at the latex gloves he was using to protect his hands during the lab to make sure they were snug, then reached into his own backpack to transfer a small remote control and a device the size of a bottle cap into his pocket. Nick did not notice—no one ever really noticed Jordan at all, which is precisely what he hoped. As the class period went on, Nick continued his out-of-character banter with a few of the students, and as he was doing so, Jordan dropped the bottle cap into Nick's backpack. When he was certain that Nick was not close enough to make a sudden move to get it, Jordan pushed the button to the remote control which was still in his pocket.

A shrill chirping sound filled the classroom and a pulsing light appeared from Nick's backpack. Nick's face turned pale, and in a state of great confusion, he panicked, racing from the room. Diaz had always been suspicious of the kid, and his sudden departure coupled with the beeping backpack put him on instant alert. He wasted no time in ordering the rest of the students out of the building. Something about Diaz's tone made them respond instantly, and they all fled immediately. Diaz, in an abundance of caution, strode across the hall to summon help from security and the administration.

These were the pre-Columbine days, but the staff was ready nonetheless. They had been trained to conduct safety drills, and within minutes the administrators cleared the building. The school's three security officers speculated that this must be a mistake, but they were not taking any chances. Diaz had already reported a concern about Nick Samuels's bomb interest to one of them, and that, combined with his police record, put the kid on the school's radar. They treated the beeping, blinking backpack as a serious matter, and before long the Greeley police, accompanied by the bomb squad, showed up.

It was close to the end of the school day, so teachers herded the students to the parking lot and buses and ordered them to go home. There would be no locker visits or practices after school. The entire school would be quarantined until further notice. The media caught wind of something happening and raced over to begin sorting through the rumors, which by this time were rampant.

A short time after the police arrived, Jordan Michaels pulled a small device from his pocket, tossed it to the pavement, and smashed it with his heel. He bent and picked it up, then slipped the pieces back into his pocket. At precisely that moment, the beeping sound and flashes from inside Nick Samuel's backpack stopped. Jordan sauntered away from the school, blending inconspicuously into the throng of noisy students thrilled with the few unexpected free minutes of the early release. No one spoke to him; no one even noticed him leaving.

Later that night Channel 9 broke into the regular broadcasting to report that several pipe bombs had been discovered in a student's backpack at Horace Greeley High School. They had been expertly crafted and could have taken many lives, and the student who built them had been arrested. Details were sketchy at the time, but sources revealed the student had mistakenly set off a signal that alerted a teacher. The student's identity was being withheld because of his age.

Jordan breathed a sigh of relief. As much as he planned to be an engineer or architect, he considered for a moment that he might make a great detective. He resolved to tell Ms. Nelson the whole story. She would keep it to herself, and no one appreciated a good story more than she did.

Chapter 24

Nelly

Nelly glanced out the window and noticed that the sun would be setting soon. A couple of the custodians busied themselves picking up the grounds, but other than that the school remained deserted. Since it was a Friday, the last day of the school year, most of the administrators and staff members had checked in at a nearby bar where they celebrated by drinking a few beers and recounting the highlights of the past school year.

A few teachers were probably already on their way to a distant country or some other summer adventure. Nelly had always liked that about teaching. In spite of unending work that extended long into the night or the mornings that began well before the dawn, the summer brought with it the opportunity for renewal.

Nelly had not revealed her summer plans to anyone, but the thoughts of what lay ahead excited her, and she decided to pick up her packing pace. She had resolved that when she left this room she would not return, so it was important not to leave anything of value behind.

She pulled the copy of the restraining order that her colleague Bernie Findlay had secured from the courts from the secret drawer. The order, dated some ten years ago, was issued to prevent Bernie's husband Scott from coming any closer than 300 yards to Bernie. Attached to the order were a dozen or so jarring photographs of the bruises he had inflicted on her.

Bernie was an incredible teacher, supremely dedicated and beloved by her students. Bernie was also a mother to three sons, all of whom had serious learning disabilities. Scott blamed Bernie for their struggles and for his own inadequacies as a man. During those times when he was unemployed, Bernie picked up the slack by teaching an overload. When he got his third DUI, she drove him to his midnight shift at the packing plant. When their children needed special equipment, she went to garage sales, then sold the items on eBay. No student or teacher had any idea of the hell that characterized Bernie's life. With no extended family nearby, Bernie did what she had to for survival.

Their marriage started out just fine, but within the first year Bernie knew that life with Scott would not be easy. On Bernie's 40th birthday some years ago, they had invited Nelly over for a barbeque, and after a few beers Scott started in on Bernie's weight. His ridicule was oppressive, and Nelly felt so uncomfortable that she slipped away as soon as she possibly could. Later Bernie apologized, making a few excuses for her husband before admitting that his temper was often explosive.

Over time, Bernie would show up to work with scratches or bruises, often labeling herself as a klutz and laughing about her clumsiness. Bernie and Nelly had a common moveable wall between their two classrooms, and occasionally they would combine their classes to show a movie or to conduct a writers' workshop. They were about as close as professional colleagues could be. Neither wanted their personal lives examined in any detail, and both were content with school talk and occasional social interaction outside of school. Like their much younger counterparts, teachers had cliques as well, and Bernie and Nelly each had their reasons for maintaining their distance from the popular group.

There are just so many accidents that Nelly could accept as real, however, so one day she came right out and asked Bernie whether she was safe. Bernie hemmed and hawed before ultimately revealing the entire drama that was her life. Nelly listened carefully, then offered help, which Bernie refused.

Eventually the beatings became more severe and no turtleneck top or long pants could camouflage what was happening. For the safety of her children, Bernie filed for an order of protection. She did all of this without telling her secrets to anyone but Nelly. Nelly recalled the day that she handed her the copy of the restraining order and photographs with a request to keep them in case "something happened."

Nelly kept tabs on her colleague, slipping her a $20 bill or a Bob Evans gift card occasionally to let her know she was not totally alone. Nelly's watchful eye was the only support Bernie had for many years, but eventually Scott got caught up in burglary and gambling, and he agreed to a divorce on the condition that he was not on the hook for any child support. Eventually he left Colorado, and Bernie's life returned to something resembling normalcy.

Nelly marveled at the grit of this woman; in all that time, the students saw only a strong, caring, professional teacher. The administrators had no idea what courage it took some mornings for her to even get out of bed. Her colleagues envied her at times because she came across as so happy and content with life.

Empty Desk

That was the thing about being a teacher that most people never even considered. Teachers, too, had their backstories, and many dealt with serious issues like financial problems, abuse, depression, and aging parents while juggling growing demands to teach, counsel, protect, and nurture an ever-increasing number of students.

Nelly paused, thinking of how often students would be surprised to run into her at the gym or the grocery store, as though she had no normal life outside the school. In some ways, these students were right; school had a way of absorbing every waking moment. Nelly herself, with no responsibilities to care for a spouse or children at home, often worried how she would manage to find enough time and resources to make the lesson plans, grade the papers, mentor the delinquents, deal with unreasonable administrators, and pay for classroom supplies.

Yet, despite a crumbling and danger-filled personal life, Bernie did all of this and more with an encouraging smile. Nelly considered her a hero and was pleased that she had won the $500 Teacher of the Year Rotary Award. No one deserved it more. Nelly removed the restraining order and the photos permanently from the secret drawer. She decided to ask Bernie whether she wanted them back before placing them carefully in the half-filled duffel bag.

Chapter 25

Jordan

Nelly tried to shake off the oppressive feeling about her colleague Bernie. To this day, she could still recall that humiliating birthday party so long ago. As she thought about birthdays and the fact her own was coming up soon, she flashed back to that one day during Jordan Michael's sophomore year when the class had an impromptu in-class birthday party to celebrate a handful of students who were all turning 16. It was a less than spectacular event, basically not much more than a bunch of cupcakes, an off-key chorus of "Happy Birthday to You," and a few remarks about how the roads would never be safe again with the celebrants as drivers. Nelly noticed that Jordan declined the cupcake and became even quieter than he normally was, and she made a mental note to check in with him later in the day.

After the last bell rang, Jordan stepped into Room 203 to pick up a copy of *To Kill a Mockingbird*. He wanted to get a head start on his semester reading and Nelly had to hunt down a copy from the bookroom. She had stopped keeping copies of assigned novels in the classroom because they always disappeared; it was better to just wait until it was time to start a unit and haul over the precise number of books needed. Budgets for departments were lower than ever, and Nelly and her colleagues got tired of digging into their own pockets to provide a complete set of books.

When Nelly returned to the classroom, Jordan was spraying the desks with disinfectant and wiping them off.

He was one of those rare individuals who could see when something needed to be done, and he took the initiative to do it.

This was long before Nelly knew very much about Jordan's entire history, but she knew enough to realize that he was likely a self-taught young man. She had encountered so many teenagers who drifted astray without a strong home life, but Jordan was clearly an exception. Nelly handed over the novel and commented that she thought Jordan would like the main character, Atticus Finch, because he was such a noble man and a great father.

Jordan remarked, "Well, I wouldn't know too much about that."

"What? Nobility or fatherhood?" Nelly teased.

Jordan managed a weak grin, and murmured, "Probably both. You see, my dad is prison right now. At least we think he is. He got in a lot of trouble with burglary and drugs, and in a way, I hope I never see him again. I have a few memories of him playing with me when I was little, but other than that, there's not much good I can say about him."

"I noticed that you looked upset in class today, Jordan. Was there something about the birthday thing that upset you?"

"The truth is that it made me think about my tenth birthday. It was the first birthday that I was going to have a party. At the time, my parents were already divorced, and my dad had been in and out of jail. This day was going to be special, though, because my mom said that my dad would be able to come to the party. I have to admit that I was excited about having both parents there together. I was going to have a store-bought cake and could invite four friends to the park close to where we were living at the time. I used to have a lot of friends then, so it was hard to pick just four. Anyway, it turned out to be one of the worst days of my life."

"What happened?" Nelly wondered if she even wanted to know. She could picture the younger version of Jordan and imagined the excitement of a real party. Nelly herself had never had a childhood party and recalled how she once imagined doing something extravagant if she had ever had children of her own.

Jordan sighed. "It started out great. All my friends got dropped off at the park, and we were playing some games that my mom made up. We had a scavenger hunt, a pillow sack race, and a hoop shoot. I remember wondering where my dad was, but Mom assured me that he would be there. In those days, I only saw him occasionally, but when I did he would bring presents and make promises about how he would take me fishing one day. I think he wanted to be a normal dad, but after he started shooting heroin, he just was never the same."

"Did you know what he was doing when you were just ten? Or did you come to understand what was going on when you got older?"

"Well, I knew more than most kids my age; it was hard not to, even though my mom tried to shield me. I used to hear them argue about him taking me for the day. He looked and acted so normal to me that I got upset with my mother for being so cautious. But the last time I was with him alone, it was scary. At first, he was running

Empty Desk

around like crazy, throwing the football with me, laughing and cheering every time I caught the ball. I remember thinking that I wanted to live with him, that it would be fun. But once we went inside the place he was living, I knew something was not right. Several guys lived there, and the place was trashed. Dad told me to go get something to eat from the refrigerator, but there was nothing in there except some moldy cheese. When I walked back into the main room, I saw my dad with his sleeves rolled up, a shoestring wrapped around his arm, and a long needle stuck in his vein. He dropped off to sleep, or at least I thought he was sleeping. Some guy showed up and started screaming at Dad for taking his stash—Dad came around long enough to order me out of the place. I left scared and crying but tried to lie about it when I got back home to my mom. She figured out that there was a problem, and from then on she never allowed me to ever go with him by myself."

Nelly pictured the frightened kid and realized that what he revealed now was likely just a fraction of the story. "So, what happened on your birthday?" she asked.

Jordan winced a little, then revealed what was clearly a painful memory. "After playing some games, my mom called us to the picnic table for cake and drinks. I remember thinking how pretty my mother looked in her shorts and tank top. Just as my friends started singing to me, my dad showed up. It was a hot day, but he had on long pants and a long-sleeved shirt, sunglasses, and a wool hat. The first thing he did was call my mother a slut for wearing the outfit she had on. Then he told me that I needed to come with him, that he had a job for me.

My mom immediately stepped between us and told him that I was not going anywhere. He started yelling and slapped her across the face; I remember seeing the blood trickling down the corner of her mouth. I will never forget the blood drops landing on her pretty white shirt. He grasped her neck with one hand and held it firmly, then ordered me to rip open the gifts to see if there was anything worth any money. My mother screamed at us all to run away and get help.

My friends fled, but I stayed and tried to get my dad to let go of my mom. I could hear sirens in the distance but by the time anyone came to help, he had knocked me out. He took off after grabbing my mother's wallet and a couple of my gifts, and I ended up in the hospital. The cops later found him, and he got charged with a bunch of crimes. After that, not a lot of kids wanted to hang out with me. I can't say that I blame them."

"Jordan," Nelly mused, "I don't know what to say. I'm sorry you had to go through this. Just keep doing what you're doing, and your future will be so much better than your past. Trust me on this."

She sensed Jordan was done talking for now, so she changed the conversation to a little small talk before wishing him a good evening. She wondered how many other of her students were wrestling with domestic abuse. Most likely too many.

Chapter 26

Nelly

The brightly colored playbill from the Las Vegas comedy club **Grins** caught Nelly's eye as she shuffled through more of the secret drawer's contents. The brochure featured comedian Josh Jackson, a former graduate of Horace Greeley High School. Now that Josh was famous, the school district liked to mention him as a success story at every public relations event.

The truth is he barely made it through high school, as his quirky sense of humor and lack of academic discipline led to a few failed classes and a rather tenuous hold on the diploma. The lukewarm grade point average never held him back, though. It wasn't Algebra II or College Composition that prepared Josh for a lucrative career, but rather his four years of salty humor, one-liners, and pranks.

Indirectly, Nelly played a role in the process; once she accidentally discovered him setting up one of his capers, but she decided to overlook it, reasoning that he was not hurting anyone or destroying any property. These kids needed some levity in their lives, and so did the hardworking staff.

Josh had managed to make a little money by betting starting in his freshman year. It started innocently enough by betting his classmates a dollar or two that he could make them laugh within two minutes. He had memorized 100's of one-liners and his deadpan expression was simply irresistible. Before long, kids tried finding someone, anyone, who could hold back the laughter. They hit up the janitor, the teachers, even the athletic director. They practiced among themselves, but nothing worked. Josh's jokes were weak, but they always worked. As the years passed, his reputation grew, and so did the size of the bets.

What kind of shoes do ninjas wear? Sneakers. What did the ocean say to the beach? Nothing. It just waved. Did you hear about the Italian chef who died? He pasta way. What did the duck say when she bought lipstick? Put it on my bill.

Nelly had to admire Josh's ability to not only command an audience, but also to make a decent chunk of change by the tender age of 17. Like many of her former students, Josh had to fend for himself at an early age. Rumor had it that his mother had run off to New York to pursue a singing career when Josh was only 10, and his dad was a lot better suited for watching re-runs on his old black-and-white television than his son.

To the immense relief of his dad, Josh managed to meet the requirements for a high school diploma. Within a few weeks after graduation, armed with a smile and little else, he started doing improv at dives in Denver. He gradually worked his way west, where he landed in the Las Vegas comedy circuit. It did not take long for Josh to break into the big leagues, and by the time he could drink legally he was doing the pre-shows for headliners at places like the Mirage and Winn. The autographed playbill in Nelly's hand came with Josh's personal phone number and a promise of a free ringside seat to watch him perform any time she came to Las Vegas. It was one of many items on her to-do retirement list.

Empty Desk

Horace Greeley High School may not have prepared him well for college, but it had provided him with a forum to hone his knack for comedy. Some of his early forays into comedy consisted of raw juvenile humor: a fart cushion on a teacher's chair, a pulled fire alarm, an authentic looking snake in the girls' bathroom. But as the boy matured, so did his concept of what was funny. Most of the time, he easily avoided detection by cleverly shifting attention to some unlikely and innocent bystander.

On one such occasion, he used the skills he acquired in the Mass Media class to rig up the school's public-address system so that whenever an announcement came from the main office, the speaker sounded like Minnie Mouse. It took a while for the administrators to realize that the distortion existed, as students and teachers alike enjoyed listening to the announcements for a change. Eventually the administrators figured it out, but no amount of detective work netted them the real culprit who messed with the P.A. system.

Mr. Rhoades, the assistant principal at the time, was a particularly grumpy 40-something who had it in for Josh. Personally devoid of a sense of humor, he had not found it even mildly entertaining that Josh had strategically placed plastic vomit all around the school when the school board members came for their annual tour. Nor was he pleased when Josh used a bottle of liquid Ivory soap to squirt students sitting in the tier below him in the auditorium.

Once, a teacher sent Josh to the office for distracting his classmates from their work, and Josh cheerfully grabbed his backpack and declared, "Gonna pack my bags and get ready for the next guilt trip," as he headed out the door.

Empty Desk

Then there was the time he released hundreds of crickets in the girls' restroom and made a video of them screaming and running out of the bathroom. Someone tattled on Josh that time, and so Rhoades ordered him to serve 40 hours of detention, a punishment that in Josh's mind far exceeded the crime. "Actions have consequences," the administrator declared, "yes, indeedy, and you are lucky I didn't expel you." The "actions have consequences" line had stuck with Josh and led him to one of his most memorable pranks.

In addition to sporting a particularly foul attitude, Rhoades also suffered from multiple allergies. He rarely could be seen without a handkerchief, runny nose, and bloodshot eyes. No Allerest or Sudafed could allay his sneezing and wheezing. With this in mind, Josh set to work on one of his more elaborate schemes. Rhoades had a small office, something that he felt was a deliberate slight. He kept it clean and uncluttered, though, a decision he attributed to his keen organizational skills.

One Thursday afternoon, Josh hid out in a supply closet until the building had been closed and locked for the evening. In those days, the school had a couple of fake cameras mounted in the hallways, and it was not protected with any alarms. The administrators trusted the lone night janitor to secure the building. As soon as Janitor Joe finished his chores and headed for the parking lot, Josh put his plan into action.

That night Josh pulled on his work gloves, threw on an old tee shirt, and got to work. Even though Josh worked solo, it did not take long for him empty Rhoades's office of its furniture. The school had a state-of-the art horticulture program, and the classrooms and multiple greenhouses were conveniently located close to the main

Empty Desk

offices. They contained enough plants and sod to landscape a football field, a virtual landscaper's dream. Josh grabbed the garden tools, wheelbarrow, sod, and plastic he would need, and headed back to the office.

He started by laying plastic carefully over the entire carpeted surface, then carefully arranging rolls of sod to fit the exact dimensions of the room. Next, he hauled in planters with towering sunflowers, purple hollyhocks, and newly blossomed tomatoes. Only then did he use the dolly and straps to place the desk, file cabinet, office chair, and book case back into their original spots.

For effect, he planted a hoe and shovel next to the coat rack, carefully vacuumed the outside of Rhoades's office, and returned all the borrowed tools to the greenhouse. Before leaving, he snapped a picture of the entire project, whistling a tune he had made up for the lyrics "Actions have consequences." Then he shut the door, making sure that it locked behind him, and headed home.

He decided against taking the bus to school the next day, preferring to walk so that he could arrive in time to catch the inevitable commotion he was sure would ensue. He was not disappointed, either. A flurry of activity circulated around the main office. A couple security officers were deep in conversations on their walkie-talkies, the custodial staff assembled in the hallway, and the administrators stood scratching their heads. Rhoades himself was on his third handkerchief and shook his head as the principal questioned him. Josh noticed Rhoades, unable to control his sneezing, accidently hurled a rather significant amount of phlegm onto the principal's tie. "Actions have consequences," Josh thought as he smiled to himself.

Empty Desk

The staff and teachers had to go through the office to get to the mailboxes, so they all glimpsed the perfectly manicured arbor that was now Rhoades's office. Most of them found it hilarious, and Josh overheard their comments as they left the office area laughing and smiling. Comments like "Plenty of fertilizer around there" or "Yup, Rhoades will need to bring his lawn mower to work" or "Time to get rid of some weeds" echoed down the hallway.

It did not take much to entertain the staff. Within a day, the offending foliage had been removed; the cleaning crew had removed the plants and sod good-heartedly, grateful for the plastic underneath that made the task much easier than they had anticipated. The administrators were clearly annoyed not just over the situation but also the fact they could not figure out who had sodded Rhoades's office. As a result, the horticulture teacher remained under a cloud of suspicion. He took it as a sort of badge of honor and enjoyed the credit he received from his colleagues, who joined in the fun.

For weeks afterwards, the staff stuck tiny bags of seeds into Rhoades's mailbox, and small garden tools would find their way into his desk drawers. Someone created a fake *Facebook* page called "Ask Your Gardener" that featured a picture of Rhoades wiping his nose and standing next to some sunflowers. Multiple subscriptions to *Lawn and Garden* appeared in the office, and coupons for mulch and fertilizer got taped to his office door.

The prank got even more attention when a few staff members put together a pool to place bets on who could use the most words related to horticulture in conversations with Rhoades. The rules were simple: the

Empty Desk

conversation had to consist of a single interaction and it had to be verified by a witness.

Once the betting pool reached $100, interest intensified. Math wizard and teacher Fred Howard was quite the gambler, so he was intent on winning the pool. At the time Fred entered the competition, the record stood at five, and the last day of the competition was Friday. On Thursday, Fred headed over to Rhoades' office armed with a tape recorder to secretly capture their conversation. Fortunately, Rhoades was in his office putting eye drops in when Fred knocked on the door.

Rhoades motioned for Fred to come in, then urged him to take a seat. Fred had the unenviable job of heading the committee to improve student attendance, so it presented the perfect opportunity for a chat.

"Hey, Dr. Rhoades, just wanted to *plant a seed* about our ideas so far on improving attendance. Do you have a few minutes?"

Rhoades was pleased that the committee had something to report, and he nodded enthusiastically.

"Well, I just *dug up* some data from the State Department. We thought we could *branch out* from some of the strategies that worked in the Cherry Creek schools. They have a different *crop* of students than we do, and in that district, they *weed out* the chronic offenders. If we could do something similar and maybe *root out* a dozen or so of our students who have only shown up a few times, that would really help. Then we could concentrate on *cultivating* some after-school activities to *graft* some more interest in our intra-mural programs. I bet we could even enlist the help of some local businesses to create some internships as an *offshoot*. What do you think?"

Rhoades never caught on that Fred was playing him; in fact, he himself inadvertently fed into the theme by answering, "Good work, Fred. Let's see if we can't get the district to help us *grow* these ideas into a workable solution."

Fred was declared the undisputed champion and pocketed the winnings—now $150—before heading out for the weekend. He would use it to finance his entry into a blackjack tournament at the casino in Blackhawk. "Not bad," he thought, "not bad at all."

Nelly laughed, remembering how nice it was to have a break from all the sports analogies. Administrators were forever encouraging them to take one for the team or to knock it out of the park. It was about time for a few new clichés. Nelly thought fondly about how Josh had so thoroughly entertained the staff, creating a motif that got the staff through the long stretch before spring break. She was thrilled that he was earning a living doing what he loved, and she knew the stories he would tell would delight his audiences. She wondered if the story of sodding his principal's office had become part of his routine in Vegas.

Chapter 27

Jordan

One unseasonably cold autumn evening, Jordan Michaels stepped outside to check on whether his mother had come home yet from work. Their well-worn black truck was not in its assigned place, and Jordan wondered if his mother had managed to pick up a few extra hours at work. She had informed Jordan that she had started taking on split shifts to garner eligibility for Walmart benefits, but as if by design, she always fell short of the requisite number of hours. She was beginning to worry about money, but remained determined to avoid applying for any kind of government assistance and the scrutiny it would bring.

Jordan had his part time job, but Judith insisted that he keep as much of his earnings as possible for college and urged him to concentrate on his studies. He sensed his mom's financial insecurity, though, so he occasionally earned a few extra dollars helping the building manager at the apartment complex with minor repairs and grounds upkeep. The manager was a real cheapskate and it infuriated Judith that he took advantage of her son.

On this night, it appeared that the residents had all retreated into their apartments. Most of the renters were folks in transition: divorcees, transplants from other states, people searching for permanent employment, displaced senior citizens, and the occasional young married couple just starting out. The complex had a reputation of being safe, but the turnover was frequent,

Empty Desk

and people rarely invested time in getting to know their neighbors.

Jordan decided to stroll around the back of the complex to see if the leaves were piling up. If so, he might be able to talk Mr. Wilson, the building manager, into hiring him to help clear the area. This part of the complex was being phased out, and the remaining residents were finishing out their leases. The long-term plan was to eliminate these two back buildings and build a large gazebo and picnic areas for the residents. Management was much more intent on creating good first impressions, so while the entrances were well-groomed, the back areas were basically unkempt.

As Jordan rounded the corner, he noticed smoke coming out of one of the first-floor windows. Jordan knew that unit well. A single dad and his two young sons lived there, and Jordan had previously recognized the tell-tale signs of drug trades: strange or expensive cars pulling up at odd hours, pedestrians with hoodies dropping by, the little boys sitting outside as lookouts, and the occasional delivery of some high-end television or computer equipment.

Worried about the safety of the two boys, Jordan broke his normal protocol of not getting involved. Making sure that his gloves covered his hands, he pounded on the outside door, but heard nothing. He felt the door; it was not yet hot to the touch. Although equipped with a deadbolt, it had not been set, so Jordan retrieved the all-purpose tool that Gramps had fashioned for him years earlier. He fiddled briefly with the remaining lock and with very little effort managed to force the door open.

Empty Desk

He immediately spotted the prone figure of the man on the living room floor, and instinctively knew the guy was likely dead. The strong smell of smoke mixed with chemicals and a couple liter bottles nearby with tell-tale brown residue and small hoses attached were all the evidence needed for Jordan to understand that the fire originated from a makeshift meth lab. Jordan guessed that the bottle protruding under the man had exploded, but he was not about to investigate further.

A quick look around convinced Jordan that the kids were not there, so he exited the other side of the apartment, stopping briefly in the adjacent hallway to pull a fire alarm.

Once outside, Jordan forced himself to stroll to the corner and head to the 7-11. He could hear the beep-beep-beep of the antiquated alarm and within minutes some shouts of "Fire!" but he did not turn around even once. He had learned long ago that people are attracted to drama like maggots to spoiled meat. His deliberate pace and nondescript clothes and demeanor would allow him once again to simply disappear. The last thing he needed was to be spotted anywhere near the scene of a fire.

Once he reached the 7-11, the night clerk, a nervous middle-aged woman sporting multiple tattoos, was busy fussing over the two little boys who had wandered in begging for something to eat. She was oblivious to the action unfolding just down the street, and instead grabbed a quart of milk from the cooler to go along with the greasy pepperoni pizza the boys were now happily guzzling. Jordan drew a huge sigh of relief as soon as he realized who the boys were. That relief was short-lived as Jordan contemplated the news they would soon face. The older boy recognized Jordan, and gave a faint smile,

Empty Desk

which Jordan returned before he turned to pour himself a cup of steaming black coffee.

The clerk had waited on Jordan before, and the two had a cordial relationship. "Be right with you," she said to Jordan as the two kids turned their attention to the donuts she set in front of them. As she rang up the coffee, she whispered, "These kiddos are starving. What kind of parents let their kids wander around hungry? I tell you what. They are not old enough to be walking around unsupervised, and this is not the first time, so I called the cops. They should be here soon, and I hope the cops put their folks in jail."

Not one to engage much in conversation, Jordan looked her directly in the eyes and whispered back, "Good." She responded by straightening her shoulders and heading back to the boys. Jordan drew an internal sigh of relief that the children would be safe and sauntered out of the store. He could hear the sirens approaching, and deliberately continued his walk in the opposite direction of the apartment complex. By the time the rescue vehicles arrived, Jordan was far from the scene, and except for the clerk and the kids, nobody had even noticed him.

He sipped the coffee as he walked and thought about how easily he could have been a kid begging for food in a 7-11. He credited Gramps with showing up just often enough to check on things, and mentally thanked the staff of his elementary and middle schools for slipping him treats or occasionally covering his school fees. He hoped the fire had not spread too rapidly and prayed that no one had been injured.

Later that evening, the fire was breaking news on the local channel. Fire Chief Jeff Fisher stated that the fire resulted in a single fatality; two residents had been sent to the hospital for smoke inhalation, but they were reported in good condition. He praised his crew for containing the blaze, and indicated he wanted to personally thank whoever pulled the alarm. This news pleased Jordan immensely, as he realized his actions had a positive outcome. The reporter specified that the cause of the fire was still under investigation, but the preliminary findings showed evidence of drugs being manufactured.

The next scene showed the interview with the 7-11 clerk. She revealed that the two boys had come in begging for food, and how she decided to call the police because she could see signs of neglect. Neither she nor the boys knew anything about the fire or the father's demise at the time of the call to authorities. But by this time, they had connected the dots, and the children had been safely delivered to the Department of Child and Family Services. The newscast ended with a rather alarming report on the rise of illegal drug activity in Weld County.

Jordan shuddered, thinking about his own dad, and resolved that if he ever had kids, they would never have to worry about having enough to eat or being in a drug environment. He turned off the television and glanced at the clock. Judith had not returned from work yet, and her absence worried Jordan like an annoying mosquito. He shook aside the concern, pulled out his sketchbook, and continued working on the drawing of Bear Lake he had started in art class.

Chapter 28

Nelly

The years passed quickly for Nelly, and as the 90's ended, the changes in Horace Greeley High School became increasingly obvious. In those early years of the 2000's, more and more students arrived from countries whose names the staff could not even pronounce. At one point, Nelly had students speaking 13 different languages within her Developmental Language Arts class.

Most of the minority students were Hispanic, many from Mexico or El Salvador. Their parents had arrived in the United States, often illegally, to work in the fields, the slaughterhouses, or the packing plants in the area. These jobs were easy to secure and paid well. Potential employers would rarely inspect documents too closely if they thought they had found hard workers.

Before long, though, former residents of Puerto Rico, Ecuador, Sierra Leone, Somalia, Syria, and Haiti enrolled as well. Many spoke several languages with uncanny fluency, putting the typical American students to shame. The influx of these new immigrants had a positive effect on students who started to realize the value of speaking more than one language. The Spanish classes were full, and another instructor had to be hired to accommodate the demand, as students realized that being bi-lingual would enhance their chances for future employment.

At times, though, the new arrivals spoke no English at all. Often students had gross deficiencies in their native language, largely a function of life in refugee camps or inconsistent access to elementary schools. Some could read but had never written anything. Others spoke with a combination of English and their native tongue. The district was not prepared for the challenge of such a diverse student population, so it did what most districts did: enroll the students and then turn it over to the teachers to figure out.

Nelly had been assigned to one such class that turned out to be amazing. She found it exciting to witness the melting pot and listen to the symphony of accents. With these students came their stories, ones that Nelly used to bridge the gaps in what the various groups knew about each other.

As she sifted through a group of photos from the secret drawer, she found a special one that brought her back to one of her treasured days as a teacher. The photo in her hand captured a classroom party, the occasion of which was the official United States citizenship of Fatima Kassim.

Fatima was a sweet, unassuming young lady who had survived unspeakable atrocities in her native Somalia prior to coming to America. Her account of thirteen months in a refugee camp was a tale so compelling that even the resident bully in the class listened solemnly as Fatima revealed the details.

As a 12-year-old, Fatima witnessed the massacre of her parents, sister Amina, and two brothers, Faisai and Abdilahi. Their only crime was her father's refusal to immediately hand over their family home to the insurgents. His brief hesitation was enough to cause a torrent of bullets to annihilate her entire family. Fatima managed to survive by pretending to be dead and hovering close to her cousin Kadija, her only remaining living relative. As the insurgents moved further down the road to demand other homes, Kadija and Fatima slipped into the woods, eventually joining other displaced people looking for food and shelter.

Eventually they connected with humanitarian volunteers who gathered the survivors together and transported them to a refugee camp in Kenya. There the two girls joined a middle-aged couple, Abdulahi and Aisha Hajisula, whose teen-aged sons had been forced to join the military. Despite rumors of many casualties among the young soldiers, the couple held out hope that they would one day see their sons again. Bound together by their tragic losses and uncertain futures, the four of them agreed to act as a family, as there were reports that complete families had the best chance for relocation.

Fatima and her new family learned to live on very little food and water. The days in the camp were long and merciless, the heat unbearable, often reaching over 100 degrees. Some days there were water trucks available, and they could fill their buckets; on other days, they had to hike 35 minutes to the central water tap, where they waited in hour-long lines and those behind them screamed at them to hurry.

The newly formed family of four did their best to keep each other's spirits up and used the materials that Abdulahi and Aisha had carried with them after being displaced to decorate the inside of their dwelling. Home consisted of a roofed structure made up of small branches and covered with UNHCR plastic sheeting. Aisha had never had daughters, so she enjoyed fashioning the "room" for the two girls. She stretched a beautiful patterned sheet that her grandmother had given her across the middle of the room. This was the best she could do to separate the dwelling into two rooms. She refused to think about her sons in harm's way and told herself that one day they would have wives of their own, and she would help them raise the many grandchildren she would have.

Fatima felt particularly intimidated because she was so young and several of the men in camp were ruthless in their treatment of the vulnerable. Her hijab and abaya could not camouflage her blossoming beauty, and as men circulated in the camp searching out some of the healthier, prettier young girls to use as sex slaves, she retreated from public view.

Adbulahi was an imposing figure and he did his best to be intimidating, something the two girls appreciated.

Within the first few months in camp, Kadija became increasingly ill. At first, she just started moving slowly and slept longer. Later, she suffered tremors and fevers, and refused to eat any of the meager rations provided. Medical treatment was almost non-existent, and even if they could secure medicine, Fatima suspected that Kadija had given up, a decision that Fatima fully understood. One night she quietly passed in her sleep, and from then on Fatima's loneliness and grief became almost too much to bear.

A devout Muslim, Fatima prayed frequently and recited her mother's favorite verses from the *Koran* daily to keep her spirits up. The camp had a school of sorts, a beat-up structure made of tar and wood. Most times it was staffed by a rotating staff of willing volunteers, but it had no electricity or plumbing. It did, however, offer something in scarce supply that was even more important: a bit of hope.

Each day at sunrise Fatima would wrap cloth around her feet since she had no shoes, then head to the school. There an incredible teacher recognized her keen mind and convinced her that one day she could be whatever she wanted. Fatima concentrated on her studies, holding unto this message, and waited.

One day her chance for relocation came about in an unexpected way. A group of missionaries from a church in the United States had committed to working in the camps for thirty days. These generous people had rearranged their lives in the states to free themselves up to tend to the medical, spiritual, and survival needs of these displaced people. They worked tirelessly to build shelters, plant crops, haul water, and provide medical care. Most of them had never been out of the United States and were unprepared for the many problems they would encounter.

One of the workers had gone out of his way to befriend Fatima. She trusted almost no one, particularly males, but something about Gary's bright smile and cheerful demeanor allayed her fears. Their relationship was not much more than a casual wave and greeting as they crossed paths, but it was reassuring to Fatima and she secretly looked forward to seeing him on her way home from school.

One day he handed her a book as she trudged back to camp, indicating that it was hers to keep. It had been so long since anyone had given her anything so Fatima was instantly suspicious; however, despite her misgivings, she clasped it tightly and looked forward to examining it more closely. Only after entering the shack she called home did she dare to open it. It was a children's book written by someone named Dr. Seuss. Puzzled, Fatima began to read *Oh, the Places You'll Go*. The pictures were so bright and colorful, the words so magical, and the message so uplifting that for the first time that she could remember, she smiled.

A short time later, an alarm sounded in camp. The refugees had become used to this; generally, it was a warning to humanitarian workers to hide or flee. Armed insurgents had kidnapped workers in other camps in the area, and somehow news traveled even without technology. Fatima stood in the doorway just as a covered Jeep swept by. Gary was driving, and he slowed to a stop and vigorously waved to Fatima to get in the vehicle. She hesitated for just a moment, grabbed her new book, then jumped into the back seat, where others told her to stay down.

She stayed hidden and listened as the Americans talked in somber tones about going back to the states and then trying to gather more resources before returning. They had not stayed the entire month, but they had been getting regular updates that their safety had been in jeopardy for some time. Fatima did not have complete command of English, but she understood enough to realize her "captors" were good people, so she relaxed a little.

Fatima was not certain how Gary and his crew were able to clear her for passage to America, but somehow, they did. She felt guilty about the children left behind but promised Allah that she would do her best to be a success in America and send money to help them. She realized that she might never return to her native country and felt a little guilty that this thought lifted her spirits immensely.

Empty Desk

Her thoughts drifted to the kind-hearted couple who had so graciously accepted both her and her cousin Kadija. She resolved to figure out some way to thank Abdulahi and Aisha Hajisula for all they had done for her.

Before arriving at the airport to board an airplane for the long trip to the United States, Fatima showered and washed her hair for the first time in many weeks. Some of the female workers had collected clean clothes and sturdy shoes for her to wear. As she dressed, she thanked Allah for good fortune. She remembered the line from her book: *Today is your day. Your mountain is waiting. So get on your way.* She pictured her family who had been taken from her so brutally and prayed that they were at peace.

These details were just the beginning of a profound tale that gradually unfolded over the course of Fatima's high school years. Fatima was assigned to Ms. Nelson's class, and the first fifteen minutes of every class was devoted to storytelling, so over time Fatima eventually revealed how she had lost her family and ended up in America. She was only one of many in the class whose journey to the states was one of pain and struggle, but her positive attitude and gritty determination to gain official citizenship set her apart from the other students.

Fatima could hardly wait until her eighteenth birthday to take her citizenship exam. By this time, she was a senior in Nelly's Senior English class, and many of the same students who learned her story freshman year were enrolled in this class as well. Fatima had carried around flash cards for months, using them to help her memorize obscure facts of American history and government. She could name all the Presidents of the United States, recite the Preamble to the *Constitution*, and even cite the most famous Supreme Court decisions. If anyone deserved to be a citizen, it was Fatima.

She arranged to take her test early in the day, then return to school. She took along her copy of *Oh, The Places You'll Go* for luck, and offered up her silent prayers to Allah. Nelly knew by the time Senior English rolled around that day, it would be official. Nelly made sure that there was a cake and punch ready and that the room decorations were red, white, and blue. Her classmates were excited, and they provided some of the fine touches: confetti, patriotic music, and tiny American flags.

Fatima had not expected any fanfare, so when she entered the classroom, she did not realize at first that the festivities were in her honor. The students cheered and clapped, shocked to see her wearing a lovely red, white, and blue hijab instead of the black one she always wore. Her jubilation heightened when a proud quartet of four— all recent immigrants themselves— sang an unforgettable version of the *Star-Spangled Banner*. There were not many dry eyes as the words "land of the free and home of the brave" hovered in crystal clear harmony.

The photo in Nelly's hand brought back the spirit of that day. Other dreamers in the room had been both envious of and inspired by Fatima's official citizenship, as they too yearned for their chance to make this country officially their own. At graduation, Fatima wore gold cords over her gown signifying her inclusion in the National Honor Society. As she walked gracefully up to the stairs to the platform where she accepted her diploma, she clung tightly to the now worn copy of *Oh, The Places You'll Go*.

Empty Desk

Nelly put the photo on the top of the pile of others before slipping them into an envelope and placing them in her getaway bag.

Chapter 29

Jordan

Jordan had been employed at Gracious Manor for several months when Matthew Stevens first arrived on his 83rd birthday. A taxi driver delivered him one evening with a couple of suitcases, a tattered briefcase, and a manual typewriter.

Mr. Stevens told intake interviewer Junie Buckwald that he was slowing down and that it was time to live someplace where he could get a little assistance. Most of the clients at the facility were already in advanced stages of physical or mental deterioration, so by comparison, Matthew Stevens appeared relatively fit. Junie was puzzled by the fact that no one had accompanied the old man. She was used to families dumping their relatives off and not showing up again, but generally the initial move-in involved a lot of fanfare.

Junie was tempted to tell Mr. Stevens to turn around and stay away. This place would take away his will to thrive. However, a check of the pre-paperwork indicated that he was financially able to pay for the limited care package for a full year in advance. His credit rating was excellent, so she knew his admission would not be tied up in government paperwork. She also knew that management would be thrilled to get someone who for the time being was low maintenance, so she filled in the remaining blanks on the forms and showed him where to sign.

Junie paged Jordan Michaels to help Mr. Stevens move his meager possessions to the tiny apartment in the far back wing of the building. Mr. Stevens had requested to be as far from the mainstream as possible, and he particularly wanted to be close to an exit. Jordan was pleased for the reprieve from mopping, and cheerfully hauled Mr. Stevens's things to the stark suite that would now be his home.

Over the first few weeks of Mr. Stevens's residence, the old man and the teenager interacted briefly a few times, but like Jordan, Matthew Stevens kept almost exclusively to himself. One day, one of the STNA's had discovered that the toilet in his bathroom had been running constantly, and the front office notified Jordan to see if he could fix it. He found his way to Room 356 and knocked quietly. He thought he heard a "Come in," so he opened the door and the serious, grey-haired gentleman beckoned him to enter.

"Hi, Mr. Stevens. It's just me, Jordan. I am here to fix your toilet."

"Hi there, young fellow. Just call me Matt. You must be here to fix that damn toilet. Come on in and do your thing."

As Jordan adjusted his tool belt and sought for the right wrench, Mr. Stevens assessed the young man. "You look mighty young to be a plumber," he noted.

Jordan smiled and replied, "I'm not a plumber. I am still a high school student. I just clean and do odd jobs around here. I know how to fix the toilet, though."

"I'm impressed. Not too many high school kids would know how to do that. Where did you learn it? Your father must be quite a guy."

Jordan got a strange look on his face, thinking of the fact that his father was likely still in prison. Ever aware of his need to keep his past a secret, Jordan just avoided the comment by flushing the toilet a few times. As he replaced the flapper, he mentally thanked his grandpa for conveying the importance of learning how to use tools.

The two continued with a conversation about the weather and the current news. Mr. Stevens seemed somewhat reluctant to let Jordan move on to his other responsibilities and kept up a steady stream of questions. Jordan recognized what he was doing. Like Jordan, the old guy was lonely. Jordan was ahead of schedule, so he accepted the gentleman's offer to "sit for a spell." When he pulled out a worn checkerboard from a drawer and invited Jordan to play, Jordan agreed. Mr. Stevens won the first game easily, and Jordan resolved to pay more attention if they ever played again.

In the following weeks, Jordan visited the old man each night he worked, saving enough time so that they could get in a quick game of checkers. The two developed an easy friendship, but initially both avoided information about their pasts. They talked about nature and religion, philosophy and ethics, sports and education. They kept a running tally of who won the checker games, and from time to time, Jordan would bring in spicy burritos from Alberto's for the two of them to enjoy.

One day the receptionist greeted Jordan with the news that Matthew Stevens had taken a rather serious fall and that he had been hospitalized for hip surgery. Rehabilitation might be a lengthy process, and he would be placed in a different area of the facility when he returned. Jordan wondered if anyone from his family would show up to help him. He had not mentioned anyone close to him, and Jordan had never asked. Injuries to the elderly could be quite serious, even lethal, and Jordan was determined to do what he could to get his friend back to his former checker-playing, smooth-talking self.

It was a couple of weeks before Mr. Stevens returned to Gracious Manor, and he did so equipped with a walker and a stockpile of medication. Jordan readjusted his schedule so that he could visit with his friend before clocking in for his shift. He knocked tentatively on door and opened it when he heard the mumbling on the other side. Mr. Stevens glanced up from his book, which he held upside down, and looked with confusion at Jordan.

"Hi, there, young man. What can I do you for?" he said. Jordan sensed something was not the same, but he smiled and said, "It's me, Jordan. Remember? We played checkers before."

"Sure, sure. I remember. What is your name, young fellow?"

Jordan swallowed hard, realizing that something was off for his old friend. He had observed a steady decline in cognitive function of many of the other residents, but he was taken aback by this sudden change in the old man. He had come to think of Stevens as his muse, and it pained him to even consider losing those long, meandering conversations about life. Matthew Stevens was the closest thing Jordan had to a confidante since coming to Colorado, and the thought of losing him was disconcerting.

Jordan's responsibilities at the nursing home had gradually evolved from dealing primarily with maintenance and cleaning the facilities to handling people. Although he had no certification and the state would yank the license of the facility if they knew, it was Jordan who often lifted the sick unto bedpans or held their frail arms to prevent them from flailing. The night workers were few, and their job descriptions often overlapped.

So it came to be that Jordan Michaels became Matthew Stevens's guide through the last months of life. It was a challenge that suited the teenager; he often thought of Gramps and hoped his devotion to this man counted for something.

Each night Jordan would appear at the gentleman's door, knock quietly, and then enter. And each night, Matthew Stevens would say, "Hello, young fellow. What's your name?" Jordan would reply, "I am Jordan Michaels, and I am here to visit with you for a while. Is that OK?"

In these nocturnal meetings, even Matthew's closed door could not block out the groans and snores emanating from the long hallways. The unnerving sounds convinced Jordan just how isolated and lonely his own life had become, so he often held Matthew's hand as the old man tried to sleep. "Talk to me, young man," Mr. Stevens would say. "What is going on out there in the world? Tell me what I need to know."

At first, Jordan would share little vignettes from his day at school or what he had heard on the radio. As time went on, realizing that Matthew Stevens would soon forget their conversation, Jordan slowly revealed all those bottled-up secrets of his young life. Once one story unfolded, the others spilled over into the confines of the tiny room. It was Jordan's therapy to confide in his friend, to separate the truth from all the lies, and to verbalize the hopes and dreams for his future. At times, Jordan would catch the old man staring intently at him as he spoke; sometimes he would grasp Jordan's hand extra tightly when Jordan revealed the dangerous escapades of his youth. Jordan was convinced that there was little cognition behind those sympathetic nods, but it was enough to be listened to by his once so vibrant friend.

One night after Jordan had told his last secret, Matthew Stevens sat up abruptly in his uncomfortable bed, and in a speech of utter clarity, he informed Jordan, "Listen to me carefully. We all have secrets, son. Don't let anyone tell you that you can't reach your dreams. You will not only get to college, but you will excel there. I know it as surely as I know that we are alive. There is an envelope under my old typewriter there; will you get it for me?"

Jordan felt under the typewriter and discovered a thick sealed envelope bearing the name and address of a local legal firm. He handed it to the old man, who fingered it extra carefully before giving it to Jordan.

"This, Jordan, is for you. Do not open it until your graduation day. It won't be long now before I am gone. I have been listening to your stories and I want you to know that I heard and understood every single word. I know you thought I could not understand or remember what you said, but the truth is that you kept me going. Your stories are remarkable, and they are safe with me. I have many secrets of my own, but for now it is best you do not know them. Lord knows, you have dealt with plenty already in your young life. The truth is when you get to be my age there is no better ruse than pretending to have dementia, and I am sorry I tricked you. Just know that you gave an old man companionship when he needed it most. Tuck that envelope away for now, young man. After you earn that high school diploma, open it up."

Jordan stammered, not sure what to think or say. Mr. Stevens indicated that Jordan needed to put the envelope in his pocket. Jordan did as he was told and when Stevens was certain the packet was secure, he grasped Jordan's hands firmly, smiled, closed his eyes, and drew one very long last breath.

Chapter 30

Nelly

Nelly had to crawl on the floor to reach into the recesses of the drawer to make sure that she had fully removed its contents. It was not quite empty yet, and the few remaining items had been stashed away so long ago that she wondered if she would even remember what they were. She located a package carefully secured with bubble wrap and tape, then recoiled just a bit when she remembered what it was. It had been several decades since she had hidden the still blood-stained 8-inch blade and black leather sheath in her drawer.

The knife belonged to the then-boyfriend of Maria Adele Gomez-Carranza, a student named Mario Ortega. He was one young man that Nelly hoped would never cross her path again. She recalled Maria fondly, though. Teachers were not supposed to have favorites, but it was hard not to when it came to students like her. She had been a senior in Honors English when Nelly first met her, and her writing skills were phenomenal. She was painfully shy, but with some gentle prodding, she was starting to blossom. She was not only articulate and kind, but also stunningly beautiful.

At that time the school had very few Latino students, and only a small fraction of them made it into the academically rigorous classes, so Maria was an exception. As Nelly thought back on that era, she had to admit that the school system itself could have done so much more to cultivate educational advancement within the Latino community. This was long before differentiated learning,

ESL classes and AVID programs worked their magic, so native Spanish speakers often ended up primarily in developmental English, industrial arts, music, and Spanish classes.

Largely due to Maria's reticent nature, she had avoided college-prep classes. Due to a scheduling mishap, she ended up in Honors English, but with Ms. Nelson's encouragement, she stayed. Up until her senior year she had never even considered college as an option; no one in her extensive family had ever gone to college and many never finished high school. She envisioned her life much like that of her mother and aunts. They were the core of their large extended families, anchoring them with strong Catholic values, hard work, great meals, and deep loyalty and devotion to their husbands. Maria was used to taking direction from the male figures in her life, and her doting father had often remarked what a wonderful wife and mother she would be when the time came.

Greeley, Colorado had experienced a sudden uptick in gang activity in the 70's, brought on by an influx of immigrant workers employed in the beef industry, tougher enforcement against illegals in Arizona and other states, and expansive wilderness patches of land prime for harvesting marijuana.

Among the gang leaders was one Mario Ortega, tagged Cobra by his followers. Nelly had seen him in the halls of the school, and noted his prominent tattoos, menacing posture and commanding voice. His older brothers were well-known to the administration, some having started their lives of crime and violence at this very school. So fair or not, Mario was considered cut from the same cloth, and he was on the administrators' radar for theft and drugs. The bad rep was well-deserved, but his unique set of street-wise skills enabled him thus far to avoid any serious skirmishes with law enforcement.

With its lack of trained security officers and reputation as a safe school, Horace Greeley High School was the perfect place for Cobra to manage a robust pot and pill business. Intermittently he supplemented this lucrative venture with the theft of valuables from some of the wealthy country club students. In those days, students rarely kept a watchful eye on their lockers or backpacks, so it was easy to grab a watch or a wallet. He had a solid connection to the local pawn shop, whose owner asked no questions of the teenager.

Cobra was smart enough to realize that he needed to maintain his status as a full-time high school student to ensure a steady money stream. So he attended most of his classes and kept passing grades in them while micromanaging his pretty impressive theft and drug ring. The country club kids were among his best customers, so he enjoyed an extra layer of protection from detection, since members of the football team did not want their pot source to dry up.

Despite his tough exterior and violent past, Mario had a singular weakness: Miss Maria Adele Gomez-Carranza. No one could blame him. Maria's thick curly hair cascaded down her back like an out-of-control waterfall, while her deep-set charcoal eyes contrasted with her full red lips and bronzed skin. Her perfectly proportioned body was nothing short of a work of art, made even more appealing because Maria was basically oblivious to her incredible beauty. One glance was all it took for Cobra to decide that he must have her as his own.

He first noticed her as she struggled down the hallway trying to balance an overloaded backpack, purse, and water bottle. He slid up beside her and flashed a friendly smile before grabbing the backpack. "Hey, you do not have to lug anything around here. Don't tell me someone as beautiful as you is a schoolgirl." *Schoolgirl* was an insult in the Latino gang subculture. It implied that a female had sold herself out to the system, that she was embracing the gringos instead of her own often male-dominant culture.

At the time Maria had no knowledge of the nuances of the word *schoolgirl*, and just saw a handsome young man willing to help her carry her backpack. She ran in much different circles than Cobra, so unaware of his reputation, she responded with a shy smile. She noticed his tattoos, but focused on his sturdy shoulders, jet-black hair, and straight white teeth. Like Maria, Cobra had a strong presence that one could not easily dismiss.

Within a few weeks, after brief conversations in the halls between classes, Cobra asked Maria out. She accepted, and it took no time at all before the two were inseparable. Despite some initial misgivings, Maria surrendered to Cobra's charms as well as his demands. He preferred that she be at his beck and call, which contributed to intermittent absences from classes and a decline in her academic performance. She stopped carrying her books and supplies, and although she came to Honors English, she was largely unprepared. One day Nelly pulled her aside for an intervention.

"What is happening? Why are your assignments incomplete? You started the year so well. What's up?"

Maria lowered her eyes and as she shuffled her feet she replied, "Cobra thinks that school is a waste of time and if

Empty Desk

I study too much we won't have enough time together. He says we will get married as soon as we graduate."

"What do *you* think? What about college?"

"I would like to go, but I don't think it's possible anyway. My family could never afford it. I'll be OK without it."

"You shouldn't limit yourself. With your brains you could be or do anything you want. Don't let this boy hold you back. I know of a scholarship that you could get that would pay for most of it. Your test scores are in the top 5% in the nation. Don't lose this opportunity; if you do, I am sure you will regret it."

Nelly paused and held back on what she really wanted to say to Maria, which was that she should dump her loser boyfriend. She chose instead to stop lecturing and inquired where Maria's books and supplies were. It was then that Maria revealed that Cobra would not allow her to carry any of these items—that it was too much of a *schoolgirl* thing.

Nelly held her rage in check and decided to offer Maria a space in a cupboard in the classroom where she could keep her school supplies until she came to her senses. Maria looked at Nelly gratefully, and from that day forward, her attendance and grades improved. She would slip into the room several times a day to retrieve a paper or book she needed for another class. Remarkably, in the classroom Maria remained a keen intellect, but when she stepped out into the hallway and into her boyfriend's waiting arms, she became something entirely different.

There was no accounting for young love, and Nelly knew full well that being too critical would be counterproductive. She felt that the best she could do for Maria was offer her a better choice, and hope that within time Maria would recognize it.

Over the years, Nelly had faced more ethical decisions than she could count. Her interactions with Maria caused Nelly more than one sleepless night. Part of her wanted to demand that Maria, and all girls for that matter, take ownership for their futures, and to rid themselves of anyone and anything that interfered with their education. Yet another part of her knew that it was not her business or responsibility to tell female students who they should love, whether they should allow themselves to follow orders from their boyfriends, or whether long-held cultural customs were now archaic.

As the school year progressed, the relationship between Maria and Cobra intensified. Like Maria, Cobra lived in two worlds: one as an elite and often ruthless leader of the Locos gang, the other as the boyfriend of a sweet and basically naive schoolgirl. The two teenagers loved one another, but forces greater than the two of them would shatter their world.

Since Maria had never been jumped into the Locos, or any other gang, she was a source of contention between Cobra and his followers. They were suspicious of her; she was definitely more mainstream and not part of the hood. In spite of Cobra's deep and unwavering allegiance to his homeboys, he did not want Maria involved and did his best to keep her away from his friends and his neighborhood. To maintain his stature as the kingpin of his gang and thus assure the lion's share of profit from his pot business, Cobra had to flex his muscles and prove that his chica would not interfere with any of the gang's operations.

The opportunity to protect his business and his woman presented itself when some of the more powerful members of Cobra's rival gang wanted in on some of the high school pot profits. They observed Cobra's devotion to Maria, and realized that his love for her was a point of vulnerability. For weeks, after-school battles over pot-selling turf raged within neighborhoods, and rumors circulated that the deciding factor would be who could survive an ultimate fight between Cobra and his chief rival Burnout. In the week leading up to the battle, Cobra kept Maria in the dark about the event. When she questioned him about why he was acting so distant, he simply told her that he had things on his mind and not to worry about it.

The showdown between the two rivals was set for a Thursday night, the designated location being the garage of an abandoned sugar beet factory. Members from the two groups assembled almost somberly, and after some brief posturing the two foes faced one another, unaware that both of their lives would change forever.

Burnout took the first punch, a massive blow to Cobra's jaw that almost doubled him over. It was a powerful first move, but one that elevated Cobra's rage, particularly since he was fully aware of the jeers of the crowd. He aimed for Burnout's nose and connected with a perfectly timed and positioned blow. Blood splattered on their clothes and rolled to the ground in tiny rivulets.

Burnout's next move was a heck of a shot to Cobra's chest, forcing him to expel some choked air and temporarily lose footing. A fury of rapidly exchanged fists put both young men in considerable pain. The audience was fully engaged now, but unwritten rules dictated that no one interfere.

The two enemies stood tall for a few brief moments, jockeying for prime position and catching their breath. Cobra had met his match, and the next powerful jab sent ripples of sharp pain through his entire torso. He shoved Burnout against the wall and grabbed his throat, where he held him a full minute before Burnout managed a quick right-left-right. Variations of this encounter continued, with neither party surrendering despite excruciating pain and mounting injuries.

Burnout knew a way to put the finishing touches on Cobra. Just when Cobra was close to passing out, Burnout sneered, "Tell Maria goodbye, bitch." The mere mention of her name was enough to launch Cobra into an uncontrollable frenzy; he had long held a nagging guilt that something could happen to her because of his circle of friends, and he was determined to protect her at all costs.

Suddenly, someone in the crowd hurled a large knife into the fray; Cobra immediately recognized it as his brother's and quickly seized it. The introduction of a weapon broke protocol but Burnout merely jeered and attempted to knock it out of Cobra's hand. "You aren't getting' outta here alive, so say your prayers," he snarled. In the commotion that followed, another blade magically appeared, and both fighters quickly realized that this was no longer a conflict over weed profit. This was now a duel to the death.

There was just a brief dance of the two rivals, both now bleeding profusely. They glared angrily at one another. Burnout got the first strike, a quick but deep slice to Cobra's chest. Using his last ounces of energy, Cobra launched himself straight to Burnout's heart, and pounced. And in that very second, the force of the thrust pierced Burnout's heart and ended his life.

In the minutes that followed, some fled in stunned realization that yet another of their own was gone. Others charged their enemies, while a few raced to make promises to the now motionless body of their leader. In the chaos that followed, amid a small army of protective followers, Cobra managed to slip away, knife in hand, not at all certain what to do next. He was now a wanted man in his own neighborhood, and within hours he knew the law would be searching for him as well. His first thought was that he would make his way to Mexico, where he might be able to locate some long-lost relatives and disappear.

His next thought was Maria. It was impossible to tell her goodbye, and he wept, knowing that she would be heartbroken. He was grateful that she had had no part in the gang and so far no knowledge of the showdown that had just occurred. He headed home, counting on the fact that his enemies would not immediately be forthcoming to the police. They would want to settle their own scores.

He took advantage of the short window of time to race to the home of an uncle. There he showered, bandaged his wounds, and grabbed some clothes and money before discarding his bloody clothes in a dumpster near the 7-11, where he stopped to fill up the gas tank. For a moment, he considered tossing the knife along with the clothes, but decided against it. It would be best to keep it until he could get his hands on a gun. He took a black sheath from the back seat of the car and shoved the bloody knife into it. Just then he spotted Maria's leather jacket, which she had accidentally left in the car. He felt dizzy but

Empty Desk

brushed the feeling aside. If he were to get away, he would need to keep a clear head.

Could he risk trying to see her one last time? What could he possibly tell her? Would she ever understand? Her home was on the way to the expressway, and he decided that he would just put the jacket on her porch. Hopefully when she saw it, she would get the message that his last thought in Greeley had been of her. In an abundance of caution, he parked a few blocks away, and grabbed his knife in case he needed it.

By now the pain of his injuries had set in, and his head was throbbing. He unwisely wrapped the jacket around the knife to disguise it and started walking toward Myrtle Street. He was grateful for the overgrown trees and shrubs in case he needed to hide. Every dog bark and muffled voice added to his paranoia that someone was following him. He stumbled occasionally, but he gripped the jacket-wrapped knife as firmly as he could with his right hand.

When he reached Maria's house, he could see that the lights inside were on. For a moment, he considered ringing the doorbell, but the sound of her father's voice stopped him. The old man would certainly answer the door, and one look at Cobra and he'd know that he was in serious trouble. No, it would be best to stick with the original plan: return the jacket and hope that Maria would know how much he loved her. He inched up the steps and just as he reached the top one, the automatic sensors lit up the entire area. He tossed the jacket unto the porch and staggered off into the bushes, where he passed out.

When he came back around, he had the faint recollection of glimpsing Maria picking up the jacket and then her father telling her to get back inside. He had no idea how much time had passed, but he rose slowly, adjusted his hoodie, and sluggishly made his way back to his car. It started without a problem and he headed south. About an hour into his drive, he realized that he no longer had the knife. Had he left it in the jacket? Dropped it in the shrubbery? Distraught that he inadvertently may have involved Maria in this mess and not wanting to call her and leave any electronic trail, he pressed the accelerator to the floor and raced down the highway.

By lunch time the next school day, word of the stabbing and death of Antonio Martinez aka Burnout circulated around the halls of Horace Greeley High School. The likelihood that Cobra had something to do with it kept the rumor mill buzzing, and his absence was noted by more than just his teachers. Nelly's immediate concern was for Maria, and she anxiously waited for Honors English, hoping that she would be there.

Maria arrived in class with puffy eyes and a worried look. She headed to the shelf where she kept her books and supplies and placed an odd-shaped package there before pulling out her notebooks and copy of *Hamlet*. Nelly glanced down, then started class, hoping that Maria did not know she had been watching her. When the fire alarm went off mid-class, Nelly watched Maria's panicked look at the cupboard before she left the room.

Something told Nelly not to get involved, but she never was one with much restraint. She had a gut level feeling that whatever the package held could keep Maria from going to college. Before leaving the classroom and turning out the lights, she slipped the unopened package into the secret drawer for safekeeping. The following Monday was the interview for the Reese scholarships, and so far, Maria was a top candidate. If her boyfriend was indeed a killer, then this scholarship could put Maria on a path far away from that brutal young man.

The students took their time returning from the fire drill, so it was pointless to start class again. When the bell rang shortly after the last stragglers returned, Maria headed over to the cupboard. After a frantic search of the cupboard, the panicked teenager turned and met Nelly's gaze. Guessing that her worst fears were true but not wanting confirmation, Nelly truthfully stated, "I found a package in the cupboard and I have not opened it. I put it away for now."

Maria glanced at Nelly with that deer-in-the-headlights look and struggled to find words. Nelly held up her hand. "Before you say anything, think about this. We don't want anything, and I mean anything, to interfere with that scholarship interview on Monday."

Maria's whole body shook. Once the first tear coursed down her face, others followed in an unbroken stream. She ran over to Nelly and hugged her tight before leaving the room without speaking a single word.

The two never spoke of the package again. Not when Channel 9 News reported Mario had been captured trying to cross over the Mexico border in a stolen car. Not when Maria signed her acceptance papers for admission to the University of Colorado. Not when a judge sentenced Mario for twenty five years for car theft and aggravated murder.

Many years later, Nelly learned that Cobra had indeed left the knife with Maria's jacket on her front porch. That night Maria did not know the story behind it, but when she saw the dried blood on the blade, she sensed the gravity of the situation. Being careful not to let her father see it and not knowing what else to do, she wrapped it up and took it to school to hide it temporarily in Nelly's classroom.

The story of the fight and resulting death circulated around school by the end of the first period. Realizing that Cobra must have been involved, Maria feared that her connection to him would lead police to her home, perhaps with a search warrant. She also did not want her parents to be put in any danger and figured that even if the police searched her locker, they would not know to look in Nelly's cupboard. She intended to dispose of it, but Nelly's action prevented that from happening.

More than once Nelly considered opening the package, suspecting its contents, but with multiple witnesses to Burnout's murder, the need for the murder weapon was moot. So here she was, decades later, holding an instrument that had cruelly taken a young life. She considered what to do with it, ultimately deciding to put it in her bag with the other items for the time being.

Chapter 31

Jordan

After living in Colorado for a few years, Jordan was starting to relax a little. School was going well, his job was more than okay, and he and his mother were still living quite comfortably in the apartment.

To her credit, Judith had kept her worries about money and potential issues at Walmart to herself. She was close to her son but was still trying to make up for her less-than-perfect start with him back in Ohio. For this reason, she held onto the Walmart position, even though it was a monumental effort most days. She was learning that there are as many jerks in corporate America as there are in drug trafficking.

One employee, assistant manager Shikira White, seemed to have it in for Judith. Shikira had spent the better part of ten years trying to secure a management position with the company. Despite long hours, impossible shifts, and inconsistent pay raises, she toughed it out in hopes of one day being promoted to a position she had rightfully earned. She pushed aside thoughts that her size, gender and race had kept her from advancing all these years. It was hard not to consider that these factors mattered whenever an attractive white woman or some middle-aged white guy with less experience received one promotion after another.

When the newest store manager, a rather awkward and overly cheerful man, assigned Judith Michaels to her department, Shikira was a little annoyed that she had to train yet another employee. However, Judith could at least read directions and speak proper English, so it could be worse. Eventually Judith's work ethic and ability to follow directions impressed Shikira, but she took Judith's reserve as snobbery. When Judith appeared for work with her perfect makeup and trim figure, and easily climbed up and down ladders, Shikira started feeling a little jealous. Before long, upper management started visiting the women's department more often and complimenting Judith for her product placement or some other ridiculous reason. When Judith received "Employee of the Month" and recognition for a suggestion on flexible scheduling, Shikira felt the pangs of a growing jealousy.

Shikira resented Judith's favored status. Aware of upper management's penchant for rewarding more attractive women, Shikira set about making Judith's work life more difficult. It started innocuously enough with remarks to management that Judith had not worn her name tag or that she parked in a non-designated employee area. Later she would change her schedule at the last minute without notification. Then when Judith showed up at the wrong time, Shikira would write her up.

Despite Judith's lack of a solid work history, she could recognize a saboteur when she saw one. Not really understanding what she had done wrong but intent on preserving her minimum wage position, she did her best to placate the resentful Shikira. She cleaned up the puke in the ladies' restroom without complaint, worked the unpopular split shifts, and willingly dragged the shopping carts from the farthest recesses of the parking lot in the pouring rain.

There really was no legitimate reason for Shikira's maltreatment of Judith; it was just one of those unexplainable, unfair outcomes of a system and a

Empty Desk

company that disheartens its core workers. Shikira realized she was being petty, and she was not particularly proud of herself. Yet there was something somewhat satisfying to dish out some of the same crap that she had experienced for so long. For ten long years, she had remained unappreciated and unnoticed by supervisors who gave her the same kind of shoddy treatment that she herself now inflicted on Judith.

Just before the busy Christmas season, one of the managers announced that he had taken a position in corporate headquarters in Arkansas. This opened up an opportunity for Shikira to advance, and although she had been granted an interview, yet again she was passed over for another candidate, a 30's-something white guy with limited experience who was related to one of the buyers. With no other viable options, Shikira stayed in her dead-end position and directed her resentment toward those who worked under her.

The primary scapegoat for her disdain became Judith Michaels. Shikira continued her harassment by a series of setups to showcase Judith's mistakes. As the busy season ended and Walmart streamlined its expenditures, several associates were laid off. Despite Judith's comparatively long tenure, she was among this group; although she received a half-hearted assurance that she would be called back, she knew it was unlikely.

Not long after Judith Michaels lost her job at Walmart and all the companies in the area were tightening their belts for the new fiscal year, she reluctantly started selling drugs to keep the bills paid. She did not want to do it, and feared getting caught, but convinced herself that Jordan should have the chance to finish his senior year at Horace Greeley High School. The school district was strict about boundaries, and a move to cheaper housing on the east side of town would mean switching schools.

It started quite innocently with a connection she had made with Tom Shales, the assistant warehouse manager at Walmart. She knew he supplied many of the workers there, and so she asked him if he had any leads on a way she could make some extra money. He sized her up, let out a low whistle, and assured her that he could find something.

"Not like that," Judith protested, "I was thinking more on the lines of a little weed, maybe some pills to deliver." Shales had always sensed that Judith had a past in the business, not because she had ever bought any of his products, but there was something about her swagger and her ability to read a customer that revealed skills inherent in the drug trade.

Since Judith had her own truck, something not true for several of his other associates, Shales immediately decided that she could become his Eaton pot distributor. Eaton was a farm community a few miles down the highway, and some of his best customers there were non-threatening and flush with cash. They were generally men in their forties who worked at the banks or agricultural supply stores and wanted to chill out in the evenings. They were the kind of customers who demanded discretion. Judith had a professional look about her; if she dressed right, she would be perfect to meet up with them at a coffee shop under the guise of a business meeting, make a quick exchange, and then disappear.

Judith never knew who supplied Shales with the goods, and she never asked. It was enough to get her rather generous cut of the profit and work a fraction of the time she had at Walmart. In fact, Judith started feeling proud of herself for raising Jordan so well, getting out of Ohio, and keeping the bills paid. Maybe Jordan would get that college degree after all.

She wondered how her ex was faring in prison and stifled the shiver that ran down her spine. No amount of time would erase the sheer terror of her days in Ohio. It was a good thing that Jordan did not know the entire truth.

Chapter 32

Nelly

Long before the LGBT rights movement became public and popular, Nelly discovered how much her gay students suffered. Their torment came in many ways, from the blatant shouts of "Faggot!!!!" as they walked in the halls between classes to subtle mockery from the audience as they gave reports in front of the class.

Nelly had a zero-tolerance policy as far as any ridicule was concerned. As she explained to her classes on day one: "The world can be cruel enough outside these doors. In this room, no one, and I mean no one, will be allowed to put down anyone else. This is a zone of acceptance, and you and your story will always be heard and welcomed." Only a few students over the years tested her on that policy, and every one of them regretted it.

Typically, Nelly felt one's sexual orientation was personal: something she did not want or need to know. Sometimes, though, in the insecure and tumultuous world of high school, it simply could not be ignored. The Christmas card from Drew Clark that Nelly retrieved from the drawer reminded her of Drew's very painful journey accepting his identity.

Nelly had learned the details about Drew's story through a series of personal writings that he shared with her. The son of very conservative and religious parents, Drew had done his best to be what they wanted him to be. At seven, he joined other little guys at pee-wee football camp and did his best to keep up. At eight, the Clarks put him in club soccer, but he was no runner and coaches rarely put him in the game. By age nine, Mr. Clark came to the realization that the odds that he would follow in his older brother Scott's footsteps were slim. At the time eleven-year-old Scott had already acquired several shelves full of trophies from a half-dozen different sports, and the whole family spent most weekends supporting him as he competed in football, soccer, or wrestling. Drew was an enthusiastic cheerleader for his big brother, but the running, tumbling, and punching nature of athletics intimidated him, and he wanted no part of it.

Instead, Drew developed a love of theater, and from a very young age he tried out for every school and church play he could. There was something exciting to him about being center stage, painting sets, learning intricate dance moves, and working with other creative kids who were part of the performances. He saw the whole process as fun, but early on his parents' lackluster enthusiasm whenever he performed revealed their disappointment in him.

To acquire the love and attention he wanted from his parents, Drew joined the youth group at the church, a decision that pleased them greatly. If he could not be a star quarterback or swimmer, at least he could serve the Lord. The real attraction for Drew was the quarterly drama performance, and he relished playing the daunting roles of characters like Moses and Abraham. Along the way, he established a reputation for being a *Bible* whiz, as he could memorize and recite verses with ease. These skills, coupled with a few community service projects, were a source of pride in the Clark household.

That pride, though, was always tempered with a steady stream of suggestions of ways he could be more "manly."

Mr. Clark rejected Drew's choice of volunteer camps. Instead of assisting the orphans with theater workshops, he ordered Drew to work for Habitat for Humanity, where he would learn to use tools, a skill he would surely need one day when he got married.

At his parents' urging, Drew asked a girl to the eighth-grade dance and another to the freshman formal. Neither experience was particularly pleasant, and Drew found himself uncomfortable and eager for the evenings to end. When his parents peppered him with questions about whether he kissed the girls and when he would take them out again, his answer unnerved them.

"Mom, Dad, I know you mean well, but I am just not interested in girls. I don't want to disappoint you, but you need to quit pushing me. If you want grandkids one day, I am sure Scott will be able to make that dream come true. What I really want to do right now is just make it through the next couple of years, move to California, and then become an actor."

"Nonsense," his father replied. "You will meet a great gal one day, some pretty little thing that will give you lots of babies. And you can't be serious about being an actor. Most of those people have no morals, and no son of mine is going to live in a den of sin." Drew looked solemnly and directly at his parents, said nothing, and headed for his room.

Shortly after this encounter, Drew met a new student at school. Tom Stapleton was the son of devout Protestant parents, and church was a significant part of their family life. Tom's dad had been transferred to Colorado from Illinois to head up a branch of a new printing company, and his first act in town was to enroll his son in Horace

Empty Desk

Greeley High School. He hoped Tom would adjust well to his new surroundings, as he had endured a fair share of cruel bullying in his old school. Mr. Stapleton was impressed with the welcome they received in Greeley, and he felt that the transfer just might turn out to be a gift from God. He loved his son beyond measure but had to admit that he was secretly a little ashamed that Tom was so flamboyant and effeminate.

Tom met his first friend in his new school in Algebra II, a class he found ridiculously easy. Mrs. Haxton assigned him to a seat next to Drew Clark, who flashed a smile and welcomed him to Colorado. They discovered quickly that they were in a number of classes together, that they both had extremely conservative parents, and that they loved the hottest Mexican food they could find. These similarities formed the basis for a strong friendship that evolved into something much more over time.

After months of agony, Drew decided to "come out" officially to his parents. He was tired of hiding his feelings from them, tired of pretending he was interested in this girl or that, tired of listening to the hypocritical youth pastor (whom Drew suspected as being gay himself). Drew's admission was not well received, to say the least. Yelling and cursing, Mr. Clark blamed the media and that lowlife fairy Tom who hung around all the time. His mother collapsed in a fit of convulsive weeping that broke Drew's heart. Accepting their son as a homosexual was out of the question, and his parents set about to find a plan to get rid of this abomination.

They started by contacting the minister at their church, pleading that he keep their concerns confidential. He agreed to meet with Drew and promised that together they would "pray away the gay." They temporarily confiscated Drew's phone and monitored his computer use, eliminating Tom Stapleton from his contacts. Then there were $50/hour after-school counseling sessions with a Christian psychiatrist. When none of this worked, and Drew refused to renounce his identity, his parents considered what to do next. Since acceptance was impossible, as a last resort, Drew was taken by escorts in the middle of the night to a week-long gay-conversion camp in Colorado Springs.

The $2000 camp fee came with the guarantee that if it did not work, the client could return as many times as necessary for no additional charge. Drew had been removed from home against his will, so he and several other young men were first taken to a secure area where armed guards ordered them to do push-ups and run laps until they were exhausted. Tired and hungry, they settled into chairs to view a disturbing movie about the evils of homosexuality. The graphic images and underlying messages were carefully contrived to produce fear in the audience. To the young men in the room, the sights and sounds of debauchery and AIDS were alarming.

The "campers" were then allowed a brief intermission to use the bathroom and get some snacks. Intimidated and afraid, they barely spoke to one another. Shortly afterwards, a group of volunteers whose children had *chosen* homosexuality entered the compound; they told emotional stories of how their children's selfish decisions to embrace being gay had destroyed their friends and families. An elderly grandmother in a wheelchair told how she had but one wish before she died: that her granddaughter would give up her sinful lifestyle and turn to God. A weeping father revealed that his eldest son had died of AIDS. The overwhelming combination of exhaustion, fear, guilt, and shame of that very first night had a profound effect on the already vulnerable young men in the room.

Drew had sized up the situation early on and determined that he would escape at the earliest opportunity. Although it was difficult, he went through the exercises without objection. In one session, he was supposed to re-enact a scene from his childhood in which his father had not been the strong person that Drew needed at the time. Using his acting skills, Drew created a fictional scenario in which his dad gotten drunk and beat his mother. Nothing could be further from the truth; his dad was a teetotaler and would never strike a woman, but Drew was justifiably angry with his dad for putting him in this position, and figured his dad deserved the insults. The session leaders praised him for his honesty and assured him that with Jesus he could overcome his deviant desire to have a man care for him.

What happened next was a traumatic experience that set the course for the rest of Drew's life. Fortunately, in spite of it, Drew figured out a way to live his life authentically, and the card Nelly held in her hands affirmed that he was healthy, happy, and content with his choices.

The session that followed the family testimonials was designed to create a sense of fellowship and brotherhood among the participants. They were told that prayers would change lives, and that they were not ever alone in their struggles to renounce the devil. To that end, the organizers had hauled several elongated boxes into the room. These boxes were painted with carefully selected *Bible* verses aimed at proving that God did not approve of their abhorrent desires and lifestyles.

As the group circled the perimeter of the room, they were ordered to memorize the passages. Leviticus 20:13 declared: *If a man lies with a male as with a woman, both of them have committed an abomination; they shall surely be put to death; their blood is upon them.* Then there was Deuteronomy 22:5 with its dire prediction: *A woman shall not wear a man's garment, nor shall a man put on a woman's cloak, for whoever does these things is an abomination to the LORD your God.*

Drew already knew most of these verses, but for every one they had selected he recalled others that epitomized his personal code of ethics and his faith. When it was his turn to recite what he had memorized, he considered substituting Galatians 5:14 *For the entire law is fulfilled in keeping this one command: Love your neighbor as yourself.* Or perhaps James 4:12 *There is only one Lawgiver and Judge, and the one who is able to save and destroy. But you—who are you to judge your neighbor?* He opted instead to conform to what he was expected to do, still intent on leaving at the first opportunity.

After the recitation of verses and a particularly virulent sermon from the "master pastor," the campers were assigned to one of the large boxes in the room. In quartets—three campers and one leader—they were told to sit down inside the boxes, which they were to imagine as bobsleds. They were to place their arms around the person in front of them, hold tight, and "feel" the strength of God's arms and those of their brothers around them. The camp leaders took the anchor seat in each bobsled, and then began a set of chants and affirmations that they ordered their team to replicate. A tape of graphic sights and sounds of howling winds, thunder, lightning, and flames enveloped the room as many of the boys wept openly. By this time, Drew was so disgusted that he considered bolting, as several of the others had already attempted. It was then that he felt the erection of his team leader Justin pressing against him and his hot breath against his neck. He whispered, "I will see you tonight in your cabin. I can't wait." Instantly repulsed, Drew felt the vomit rise in his throat. "I am going to be sick. Please let me out," he yelled.

He stood up, and a couple of the other leaders ran to him to assure him that it was just the devil leaving him. They accompanied him to the restroom, and afterwards praised the hard work he had done. Flanking him on either side, they escorted him back to the bobsled room, where he saw a smiling Justin gesturing for him to return. He faked a collapse, so the pastor allowed him to remain seated on the side until the session was over.

While Drew contemplated what to do next, he decided the best chance for him to escape was to get word to the outside world. There was no way he was going to spend a night here, let alone get within twenty feet of Justin. He knew his chances of being sexually abused were imminent and he worried about the other campers, most of which were younger and more vulnerable than he was.

He considered trying to get word to his parents about what had happened but realized that they would never believe that one of the Christian leaders would behave improperly. He could just hear his dad's voice telling him that he was weak and deceitful. Instead, he concocted a ruse to get word to Tom about his demise and prayed that Tom would be able to help him escape. He approached the master pastor with a request to speak to his father; using his best acting skills, he told him that it was his father's birthday, and that he wanted to give his father the best present of his life: renouncing homosexuality. The pastor was thrilled that the conversion therapy had been successful so quickly, so he agreed to let Drew use his phone to call his father. Of course, the call would have to be monitored.

Drew trembled as he dialed Tom's number. Tom picked up immediately, with a rather frantic, "I was just thinking about you. Are you okay?" Drew broke in quickly with the words, "Don't talk, Dad, just listen. We are on speaker, and the pastor is right here with me. Sending me to gay conversion camp was the best thing you could have ever done. I know today is your birthday, and I just wanted to give you a present. I have accepted the word of the Lord, and I promise that I will fight the devil every day from here on out."

Tom understood the message, and then did exactly as Drew had hoped. With his strong, authoritative voice, Tom assumed Mr. Clark's role perfectly, "Drew, I can't tell you how happy you have made me. I can't wait to tell your mother. Actually, I was not going to tell you this until you returned from camp, but your mother is in the hospital. She took a bad fall and is in surgery. She will be fine, but now that I know you are on the right track, maybe this might be a good time for all of us to be together." Tom paused, and Drew broke in with, "Oh, Dad, I am so sorry about Mom, and I really want to be there. Is Scott back from college? Can he come get me? Please, please, Dad. I want to be there for Mom."

Without skipping a beat, Tom asked to speak to the pastor privately. Pastor Schelling took the phone off speaker and engaged in a rather lengthy conversation with the person he thought was Drew's father. While Drew sat and waited in absolute agony, he started shaking uncontrollably. This turned out to be a fortunate turn of events. The pastor noticed, and not wanting a sick kid on his hands for an entire week, he let Mr. Clark know that perhaps releasing Drew early would be a good decision.

The pastor put the phone back on speaker so the three of them could pray together. Mr. Clark then assured Drew that his brother Scott would be there in a few hours to pick him up. He asked the pastor the exact address so he could program the GPS, which he readily provided. Pastor Schelling inquired what kind of vehicle Scott would be driving. Tom gave the description of his car, and in a stroke of genius, asked if Shelling needed a license number. "No, sir, that will not be necessary, but I appreciate you understanding how discreet we need to be in our operation. I think this has come to the best outcome possible, but if you want Drew to come back to camp, or to attend another in the future, remember there will be no charge." The three exchanged good-byes, and Drew ended the conversation with a tearful, "I love you, Dad. Tell mom I will be there tonight."

The next two and a half hours passed slowly. After Pastor Schelling clued Justin in about the turn of events, Justin offered to sit with Drew until his ride came. Drew spoke up quickly, "No, that will not be necessary. If it is okay, I would just like to pray and read the *Bible* in the office. I think I need a little time alone right now." Schelling thought this was a perfect solution, as he did not want to take Justin away from the many boys who needed his spiritual guidance that day. Often the first day in camp resulted in significant breakthroughs, like the one Drew Clark had just experienced, and they needed all hands on deck.

Drew's exodus from the venue went smoothly. As soon as he spotted Tom's car entering the camp, he shouted a relieved, "My brother is here. Tell Pastor Schelling I appreciate everything he did for me," to the volunteer secretary in the office. She stood up and checked the note Schelling had given her. Satisfied that the driver was indeed a member of Drew's family, she wished the boy well and returned to reading the novel she had started that morning.

What happened in the months that followed was a novel in itself. The Clarks refused to believe Drew's allegations of sexual imposition and accused him of unspeakable acts with Tom. After months of pleas, prayers, promises, and arguments they issued an ultimatum. Unless Drew renounced identifying himself as gay, and unless he stopped any association with Tom, he was no longer their son. A heartbroken Drew cut all ties with his parents, then moved into an apartment with Tom, who had borrowed against his trust fund to support them until graduation. Except for an occasional text from his brother Scott, Drew never heard from his family again.

Despite all this chaos during his senior year, Drew worked courageously with a *Denver Post* reporter to expose the horrors of Colorado's gay conversion camps. A Hollywood producer was so interested in the story that she contacted Drew about starring in a movie about his involvement there. Ironically, Drew's lifelong dream to be an actor unfolded from his painful personal experience at the retreat.

Nelly opened the Christmas card from Drew, and read the words her former student had written: *Thanks, Nelly, for listening to me and accepting me when I needed it most. Life is good. When I make it to the Oscars, I hope you will be my guest.* Nelly thought about what an honor that would be as she slid the card into her waiting bag.

Over the years, his notes to her revealed mostly positive messages about an exciting and successful life as an actor in California. Drew and Tom were still together, and they even talked of adopting children. But she could sense some sadness too. Drew had hoped that his parents might have a change of heart and come to the opening of his first movie, but the invitation had been returned with the word REFUSED scrawled across the envelope. There were just some stories that Nelly would never understand, and this was one of them.

Chapter 33

Jordan

Jordan entered Nelly's empty classroom just as he had so many times before. Nelly was normally happy to see him, but on this day, she was exhausted, and dreading the mountain of ungraded papers she had just packed into her briefcase. One glance convinced Nelly to set everything down and talk to him.

"What's up?"

Jordan shuffled his feet and mumbled something Nelly could not understand. He looked a little worried, so Nelly pulled out the rocking chair and motioned for him to sit down. He perched at the end of the chair, hesitant to ease into it fully, almost like he feared he would never be able to get out of it again. Nelly knew that feeling. The chair had often served as Jordan's confessional over the years. Now that he was a senior, and Nelly had heard so many chapters of his very complicated life, she wondered what more she could possibly learn.

On this day, though, he wanted to share his concern for another student. "I just wanted to talk to you about the poetry that Gail wrote for class today. I was her peer reviewer and it was some heavy stuff. It was all about being alone in the world and being made fun of all the time. She thinks that because of the way she looks that she doesn't deserve love. It sounds, to be honest, like she wants to kill herself."

Empty Desk

Nelly had also noticed the change in Gail, once so positive and involved in class discussions. Over the past few weeks, though, she had retreated more and more into herself. In fact, Nelly had deliberately chosen Jordan to be her peer reviewer because she figured he would be kind as well as honest in commenting on her poetry. Before pursuing the matter further, Nelly mentally reviewed what she knew about signals that someone was serious about suicide.

She was careful not to discuss her perceptions of Gail with Jordan. Even though Nelly trusted Jordan, she had never considered it appropriate to engage one student in an analysis of another. "I have not yet looked at her work, but I will do so tonight. Did she say she was thinking of suicide? Did she mention any method or weapon? Have you noticed anything out of the ordinary in her behavior?"

"Just read it, Ms. Nelson. It is real scary. I think she means it—she sounds absolutely hopeless. That one poem "Better Off Dead" sounds like she is talking about herself. She was always nice to me when I was new to this school, and if I had close friends, she would be one. She has changed lately, and I don't know how to help. She has started ditching Algebra and French, and I saw her crying at the bus stop. I think she just comes to Poetry class because she likes to write."

Nelly contemplated what she had just heard, and then marveled at the young man sitting in the rocking chair. There were hundreds of great high school kids, but most of them would not bother to be terribly concerned about a fellow student who seemed depressed. Jordan had his own issues to deal with, but here he was, intent on helping someone else. To the vast majority of the Horace

Greeley school community, both Jordan and Gail were nothing special. Neither one had any friends to speak of, nor were they engaged in any significant way in the many clubs and activities the school offered. Yet they both were so gifted, one a kindhearted and hard-working survivor, the other a talented writer and keen intellect. That's the irony of high school; appearance and reality were polar opposites far more often than most people realized.

Gail was plain, quiet, and at least a hundred pounds overweight. If she were male, it probably would not be as much of a problem, although even obese teenaged boys took their fair share of ridicule. The girls, however, got fat shamed in ways that few adults could even imagine. To fit in, even the good students indulged in actions like an exaggerated step aside to hug a locker to make room for her to pass. They noted that she headed for a table in the back of the room rather than trying to fit into the student desks which were designed for average-sized students. Some would even exchange eye rolls and laugh as they quietly whispered fat jokes, and they almost never spoke directly to her. For students who did not have the right look in high school, no matter how hard they tried, there were days they might as well not even show up.

The tormentors were the same kids who would never think of making racist remarks, and most prided themselves on their liberal social consciousness. In part due to the media, but mainly because of the innate self-centeredness of youth, they engaged in these actions without regard to consequences.

Teachers witnessed these slights often, and did their best to confront them, but parents rarely had occasion to observe these behaviors firsthand. If they had, they would be horrified that their sons or daughters could be so cruel.

Empty Desk

Over time, these insults were no longer innocuous, and they gradually carved away at the self-esteem of some of the most promising young people. Nelly figured that this was what had happened to Gail, and she was grateful that Jordan cared enough to report it.

"Jordan, thanks for bringing this matter to my attention. I will do what I can, but in the meantime, just keep on being her friend. It is probably what will help her more than anything I can do."

Jordan eased back into the chair and sighed. He seemed relieved that he had said something, but Nelly could sense that there was more to it. "Is there anything else?" she asked.

"One of her poems was about watching everyone else go to a dance but being paralyzed and only imagining what it would be like to get dressed up and move to the music. The homecoming dance is on Saturday, and I was just thinking…umm…. Is it is too late to ask Gail to go? I mean, it's not a pity date or anything. I really do think she's cool, and I know neither of us has ever been to a dance. I don't want her to get the wrong idea, and I don't want a "girlfriend" girlfriend. I just don't want that poem to be her story. And I don't want her to think I asked her because of the poem, but I kinda am. Not really, though. Gosh, I don't know what to do." He stopped talking once he realized that he was rocking vigorously back and forth in the chair.

Nelly laughed. "This could make all the difference in the world. I think it's a great idea. It is a little late, but I bet she will understand. I can look up her phone number. If you call her tonight, and she accepts, there is still time for her to get a dress to wear. Tell you what—if she agrees to go, I will spring for the tickets."

Jordan shifted in the chair, then smiled. "That would be great. I will let you know tomorrow what she said. You are the best, Ms. Nelson. Thanks for listening to me again." Nelly consulted her course roster, jotted down the number, and handed it to Jordan. "Now get lost, Jordan. If I don't get out of this place soon, it will be dark outside, and I still have a lot to do. I hope Gail realizes what a dear friend she has in you."

Jordan took the number and offered to carry Nelly's briefcase to the car. The two left the building together, one to grab a glass of wine and grade some papers, the other to ask a girl to a dance and save her life.

Somewhere in Nelly's drawer was a picture of Jordan and Gail from that homecoming dance. On that occasion, they both smiled broadly. Gail looked lovely in a pale green taffeta dress, and Jordan was incredibly handsome in the dark suit and classic red tie he had borrowed from one of the old guys at the nursing home. On that magical evening, Jordan and Gail did something that most high school students took for granted but that the two of them had missed for far too long: *they had fun.*

Chapter 34

Nelly

As she continued to clear out the contents of the secret drawer, Nelly came across book one in the *Bob Series for Beginning Readers*. Nelly thumbed through its ten pages, recalling how the series had magically transformed the life of her former student Dan Norkowicz. Designed for preschoolers, the books were expertly designed to engage emergent readers through step-by-step word acquisition, phonics, and delightful illustrations. Dan had autographed the last page with a particularly heartfelt note of appreciation and a giant smiley face.

Dan was one of those incredibly likeable kids whose positive attitude, open mind, and sense of humor transformed a classroom. Except for math and music, he was not strong at all academically, but he had managed to pass enough classes to make it through middle school and land in Nelly's ninth grade Remedial English class. Most of the students in that class were just biding their time until they would drop out and start their lives on the streets; several were already wearing ankle monitors, having been court-ordered to attend classes. Others, for various reasons and despite high intelligence, just plain hated school. Dan contrasted mightily with this cast of characters, but Nelly vowed not to give up on any of them before the semester even got rolling.

If a teacher ever needed a reason to quit, Remedial English Fall Semester 2002 Section 2 at Horace Greeley High School would seal the deal. Abraham, one of the more vocal members of the class, often shouted profanities for no reason. Issac had to be seated in a separate area from the other members of the class; he had been charged with several counts of violent behavior, and the court thought that being mainstreamed back into school after an extended stay in "juvie" would help him. However, he came with the recommendation for "subtle separation" during the probationary period. As if these two were not enough of a distraction, Nelly had to keep a particularly watchful eye on Luke, who drank, and Mary, whose attire was a walking advertisement for hooking up. The irony that so many of these kids had Biblical names and the presence of kindhearted Dan were about the only reasons anyone had to smile that semester.

When Nelly thought back on the entire experience, she felt guilty that she had not noticed Dan's inability to read. It was easy to miss in some ways. Dan had developed a number of coping skills to camouflage the fact that the printed page was indecipherable to him. He could carry on a discussion on virtually any topic, he picked up minor details from films that the casual observer would miss, and he filled in the blanks on multiple-choice scantron forms with enough right answers to pass most of the time. He had a gift of calculating when he might be called on to read aloud in class and resorted to either taking the hall pass to the bathroom or coughing excessively. Several times he reported trouble with his contacts. To a teacher with a reasonable class size of reasonable students, his secret would have been detected much earlier. However, while balancing the significant demands of this particular group, Nelly did what so many of Dan's former teachers had done: she missed it.

During one incredibly stressful class period, Mary started yelling, "Nelly, Nelly, I need to change my tampon. I need the hall pass. NOW." Completely floored by her unabashed candor in a mixed group, Nelly could not believe what she had heard and incredulously said, "What did you say, Mary?" Before Mary could repeat her unfiltered comment, Abraham piped up with, "Are you deaf? She needs to use the shitter. She's on the rag." The entire class snickered as Nelly silently handed over the hall pass, which she kept under lock and key to avoid it being stolen once again.

Just then, a new student entered the classroom with the required paperwork indicating his enrollment in the class. Nelly scanned the room, unable to locate a single empty desk. *NNNNOOOOO!!!!!* thought Nelly, *I can't accommodate one more kid. Not today.* She did her best to be gracious and glanced at his name: Jesus Gomez. The irony of that name was not lost on Nelly. *Jesus*, she thought, *we really need you here.*

Later that same class period, Issac started throwing paper airplanes at Dan, who at first batted them away with a good-natured grin. Fed up with the distraction and childish behavior, Nelly demanded that Issac pick up his mess. He was unwilling to do so, so Nelly ordered him out into the hallway. There he sized up his teacher, cleared his throat, then heaved a loogie the size of Texas on the wall. "Lick it up, bitch," he taunted, as it oozed slowly down the brick wall.

Nelly was usually in control, and she rarely came unglued. This, however, was not one of those times. Maybe it was sheer exhaustion or maybe the stress of so many kids with so many issues, but at that moment, Nelly lost it. Her outrage erupted and with full fury she slapped the insolent, bulky 6' 3" teenager squarely across the face. The action stunned both Issac and Nelly. It even startled a student walking nearby; she scurried to the closest exit, not wanting to be caught up in a crazy teacher's wrath.

The truth of the matter was that Issac was not beneath fighting a teacher, but the fact she was a woman and significantly smaller than he was kept him in check. He started swearing like a drunken sailor and threatened to burn down her house, so Nelly hauled him down to office and deposited him in the principal's office. There he fumed in his chair as he waited for Mr. Rawlins to return, the imprint of Nelly's handprint flashing like a beacon across his sixteen-year-old face. Concerned about leaving her class from hell alone much longer and realizing that she was guilty of assault, an extremely distraught Nelly headed back to her classroom.

Once she entered, she immediately noticed Dan hovering over Joseph, a classmate who had already completed the questions from the day's reading assignment. It did not take a rocket scientist to conclude that Dan was cheating, and Nelly groaned, loathe to reprimand about the only kid in class who had never been a discipline problem. She told Dan to stop what he was doing immediately, and to do his own work. "See me after school, Daniel," she said. "We have some things to discuss." Ashamed, Dan nodded and headed back to his seat.

Nelly went about her day, but in the back of her mind, she worried that she might have jeopardized her job by slapping Issac. She also felt bad about embarrassing Dan in class, as well as letting Mary off for being so inappropriate. For now, though, she decided to power through the day. Sure enough, by 8th period she received a note from Principal Rawlins requesting her presence at a meeting with Issac and his parents.

The meeting started with the principal's usual speech about the high behavior standards that were the "foundation of Horace Greeley High School." He reminded Issac how spitting on a wall and swearing at a teacher were grievous offences, and that they carried consequences.

The parents exchanged eye contact before Issac's dad started in on Ms. Nelson. "So, you think it's okay to hit your students? Don't be giving me that bullshit about high standards. You are an abuser and I am going to get a lawyer and sue you for all you are worth. Good luck ever finding another teaching job." Issac perked up immediately, a little surprised that his dad took his side, while Principal Rawlins simply retreated to his normal passive-aggressive stance.

It was up to Nelly to address the elephant in the room. Summoning what courage she could, she stood (remembering from some former communications course that this would put her in a position of power), then faced Issac. "Issac, I hope you will accept my apology for striking you. I was wrong. Mr. and Mrs. Erickson, you have my assurance that this will never happen again."

When no one responded, Nelly continued, "As for a lawsuit, Mr. Erickson, filing one is certainly your right. But you should get a really good lawyer, because I intend to find a better one. If you think it is acceptable for your son to call his mother or his teacher a *bitch*, then order her to lick up his phlegm, then by all means sue me."

She paused for dramatic effect, harnessing the rising adrenaline as Rawlins shrunk into the folds of his chair, tiny beads of sweat multiplying across his face. With no support from her administrator and with mounting anger at his silence, she resumed her rant, "I am willing to bet my career that any judge in the land will understand that Issac here crossed the line and bears responsibility as well. Now, if there is nothing else, I have students waiting in my room."

She turned to Issac and extended her hand to shake his, which he did with the utmost of respect, "I hope we can put this behind us, Issac, and I look forward to seeing you in class." With that, Ms. Nelson swept out the room, shutting the door firmly behind her before racing to her classroom to vomit.

And vomit she did. The enormity of what she had just done overcame her. Not only had she assaulted a student, but she had also threatened a parent. She wondered if she would lose her job. As she tried to calm her jagged nerves and collect herself, she spotted Dan sitting patiently in the back of the room. Although she had told everyone at the meeting that she had students waiting, the fact was that she had totally forgotten that Dan was supposed to report to her after school. Being the nice kid he was, Dan asked her if there was anything he could do. He was pretty grossed out by the smell and the whole spectacle, though, and hoped he would not have to take a single step closer.

"Dan, I have had a rough day," she said softly. "I am sorry you had to see this. Just give me a few minutes to get settled." She pulled the plastic bag from the trash container, clinched it firmly, and set it aside. Fortunately, Nelly kept an ample supply of mints in her desk for those times when students' bad breath overwhelmed her. She popped a few of them into her mouth before offering some to Dan.

Nelly was still distraught but turned to Dan to give him her full attention. "OK, kiddo," she said, "What is going on? You are my star pupil, the best behaved, the strongest contributor to class discussions. Why in the world would you copy your homework from someone else?"

Dan shuffled his feet nervously before taking a very deep breath, squaring his shoulders and then confessing the secret he had concealed since second grade. "I am going to tell you the truth, Ms. Nelson. I can't read. I am fourteen years old, and I never learned to read." As soon as he said it, Nelly could sense just how painful this secret had been. Her first inclination was to deny that it was even possible. Silently she thought, *Of course you can read. You might not be an expert reader, but you could never get this far without knowing how to read.* She stopped herself from speaking, though, realizing that the whole time Dan had been in her class, *she* did not know.

Dan was emotional, trying to disguise his feelings with a few flippant remarks. Nelly asked, "Would you like to learn how?" "Ya," he stammered, "more than anything else in the world. Would you teach me?" The emotions of the entire day consumed Nelly at that moment and she lost her composure, breaking into a combination of shuddering and gasping for breath. At first poor Dan thought that his reading deficiencies had caused a nervous breakdown in his teacher, but she assured him otherwise.

Nelly recovered as best she could, apologized, and promised Dan it would be an honor to teach him to read. It was reprehensible that this wonderful young man had somehow slipped through the educational cracks, but he had. Nelly, still upset from the experiences of this day, could not blame someone else. Perhaps far too many of his former teachers had also been beset with very real

Empty Desk

obstacles like lack of discipline, poverty, overloaded classrooms, court-mandated attendance for thugs, or lack of funding.

Nelly fixed a steady gaze at the young man in front of her. She had the fleeting thought that if she lost her teaching job, she would have plenty of time to tutor him.

Here is a problem I can actually help solve, thought Nelly. *We just need a plan.* The two got to work, spending the next half hour hashing out details. Dan filled Nelly in on his early school years, the many moves his family made, the absence of any books in his home, the refusal of his father to let him be tested for learning disabilities, and his keen ability to work around being able to read. It was an amazing story, and quite a testament to the adaptability of the young man who sat in front of her.

In spite of his willingness to confess to Nelly his inability to read, Dan wanted a guarantee that no one else would know. Nelly reluctantly agreed to keep his reading deficiency in confidence but assured him that his other teachers would be equally as supportive. For the time being, it was enough that only she knew, and they agreed to start at square one. That first step was the *Bob Beginning Reader* series, and the book Nelly pulled from the drawer marked the start of Dan's long but highly successful journey to literacy.

What neither Dan nor Nelly knew was that Principal Rawlins had eavesdropped on their entire conversation. He had been about to call Ms. Nelson back into his office to scold her for her display in front of Issac's parents; he was thoroughly annoyed that he had yet another fire to put out with a set of parents. However, when he hit the contact button for room 203, he caught the sounds of a student revealing his inability to read, and Nelly's reassurance that he could learn to do so.

There was no mistaking the genuine empathy in his teacher's voice, and the fact that she was willing to help him on her own time made Rawlins rethink his anger. The entire exchange put this teacher's job into perspective, and he decided that rather than reprimand Ms. Nelson that day he would do whatever he could to support her.

The very next day Issac showed up to class with a better attitude, a handshake, and a declaration: "I think it was awesome how you stood up to my old man, Ms. Nelson. I am sorry. Really." "So am I," said Nelly.

She never saw his parents again after their initial encounter, and Rawlins avoided mentioning the incident. Much to Nelly's relief, no lawsuit ever materialized. The story lover in her, however, wondered what happened after the Ericksons left school that day. She knew there must be a lot more to this narrative, but this time she was content to just let it go.

Chapter 35

Jordan

Jordan entered Nelly's room just as she was packing up to head home. By now, Jordan was well into his senior year, and he sauntered into Room 203 like it was his home. In many ways, it was as comfortable to him as a pair of his favorite blue jeans, and he took a personal pride in the place. After all, most of the nuts and bolts of the space, from projector screen brackets to hand-made cupboards, were the result of Jordan's workmanship.

Nelly had not talked to Jordan for a while and realized that she missed their chats.

"What's up?"

Jordan shuffled his feet a bit and pulled out the rocking chair to sit down. He eased his robust frame into its waiting arms, and sighed heavily.

"Are you busy? Do you have a few minutes?"

Asking teachers if they are busy is one of the most insulting questions possible, but Nelly knew Jordan was simply being polite and she took no offense. She thought for a moment about the upcoming department meeting, the budget report, the hundreds of papers demanding her attention.

"Not too busy for you, Jordan. By the way, you aced that literature exam. Great job."

"Thanks."

Empty Desk

After a few quick assurances that Nelly had time to listen, Jordan told Nelly all about his college applications, scholarship searches, and letters of recommendation. He was undergoing the typical senior stress, basically freaking out about getting everything done well and on time. Nelly could not help but think about how far he had come from that frightened little freshman to the mature and articulate young man who now sat before her.

Jordan told her about his struggle to choose between Colorado State and the University of Colorado, as well as some of his concerns about his mother. Once he started talking about family, he brought up Gramps, who by now Nelly knew quite well from nearly four years of Jordan's stories. On this day, though, he missed him something fierce, as it would have been his 80th birthday.

"What is your favorite memory of him?" Nelly asked as she pulled a Coke from the mini-fridge. Their habit had long been to split a soda whenever they had one of these afternoon chats. Like a well-practiced team, Jordan reached for a cup and poured it half full and handed it to Nelly. Both took a sip, then Jordan started reminiscing.

"Gramps always knew how much I loved Michael Jordan. He was never one to follow sports or anything like that, but he always said that he must be special if I liked him so much. He would ask me to read to him, and I often chose articles about the Chicago Bulls or the Boston Celtics or MJ himself. I would update him on his stats and how he had personally raised attendance at NBA games. Gramps even fixed me up a basketball hoop and a little playing area near our mobile home. We practiced jump shots whenever he came around."

Empty Desk

Nelly listened as Jordan filled in more details; she could picture the young Jordan (then David Martin) racing around the net, attempting fancy jump shots, and interacting with his grandfather.

Jordan continued, "Well, one day Gramps showed up and asked my mom for the keys to the truck. He hardly ever used it, but I think he still had a driver's license and everything. Like I told you, he pretty much lived in the woods, but this day, he was kinda dressed up. He had on clean jeans, a nice tee-shirt, and he had even trimmed up his beard. He told me we were gonna take a little road trip, but I could not ask where we were going. It was going to be a surprise."

Jordan took a quick sip from his soda, then continued, "He made me pack up an extra set of clothes, and when I got in the truck I noticed that he had a cooler in the back of the truck. I thought maybe we would go hunting or fishing somewhere, so I was surprised when he headed to the highway and we passed towns like Marion, Lima, and then Fort Wayne, Indiana. What could we possibly be doing in Fort Wayne? Gramps chuckled as he pulled into a truck stop and filled up with gas. He opened the cooler and handed me some jerky and a couple oranges. We ate our lunch, then got back on the road. For a while we listened to a country station and sang along. I must have gotten tired and fell asleep. I don't know how long I slept, but when I woke up I was in a parking lot and there were hundreds of people all walking toward a huge building."

"Where were you?" Nelly asked, by this time totally caught up in Jordan's story.

"That's the best part. I suddenly realized that we were headed into the United Center in Chicago. Everywhere I looked people wore red and black jerseys. They had Chicago Bulls caps on, and some were already cheering before we even got to the entry. I don't think I have ever been that excited in my whole life. We were there, and it was real!"

Nelly pondered what this once-in-a-lifetime experience must have meant to a broken boy who had known so much chaos in the early years of his life. She mentally thanked Gramps, who by this time she felt she knew personally.

Jordan continued, "I never knew how or where he got the tickets, but once we got inside, he took me to gift shop and bought me a jersey. He would not let me look at the price tag, just bought it, just like that. I could not believe it. I had been stealing food from the store by school just so Mom and I could eat, and here he was shelling out a bunch of money on an expensive jersey."

He paused for just a moment before revealing the best part of the story. "Anyway, we had amazing seats, just to the right and a few seats up from the bench. And Michael Jordan was so close I could almost touch him. He looked right at me and smiled. I thought I was gonna die right then and there. You shoulda seen him play. It was like watching a dream. He ran like crazy, swooped, hollered, dove for balls, slam dunked a few, and his sweat poured like rain. I never wanted the game to end."

For the next fifteen minutes, Jordan described the game in vivid detail, from the subtle shifts of weight in the players as they tried to deflect a defender's attention to the instinctual moments of taking impossible shots. He relived every glance, each flick of the wrist, the brief leans to the right or left, even the wiping of their brows as players competed for the win. He knew every Chicago Bull player by name and by reputation. He described the rowdy crowd as they rose in hushed amazement or indignant protest. For a few minutes, it was as if they were both transported back to those magnificent moments so long ago.

Then Jordan recalled the ultimate memory maker. "Late in the fourth quarter, a ball sailed across the court and MJ jumped to catch it. He missed, and it struck me in the shoulder. It was incredible. I think I was on tv and everything. After the game was over, MJ caught us as we were stepping down from the bleachers. He asked me if I was OK. There I was, and Michael Jordan was talking to me!!! He saw my jersey and asked me if I wanted an autograph. I could not believe it. My very own signed jersey."

Nelly looked at the young man in front of her, happy to have heard this joyful story. In their four years together as mentor and student, Nelly had listened to many chapters of what made up Jordan's life, but she could not recall one that carried the sheer happiness that he had just conveyed. No wonder he needed to talk; on the day that would have been the 80th birthday of the dear man who helped Jordan become a true survivor against the odds, Jordan was feeling justifiably nostalgic. Nelly was glad that she had not brushed him off to grade some papers. Besides, he was a senior now, and before long he would graduate.

However, that was nowhere near the end of the story. Jordan explained how Gramps did not like staying in any motels, so he told Jordan that they would just pull over to a rest area for the night. Jordan was still so excited from the events of the day that nothing else mattered. Gramps said that he would drive for a bit, though, until he got tired. Overcome with the emotions of the day, the two began their trip back to Ohio.

They spotted a sign indicating a rest stop coming up in 21 miles and decided that they would stop there for the rest of the night. Just then, they noticed a family in a battered, broken down station wagon stopped on the side of the highway.

Gramps immediately pulled over and asked if he could do anything to help. A woman in the passenger seat was crying, as were the three young kids in the back seat. A man was kicking the ground and swearing in frustration as he pounded on the hood of the car. At first Jordan thought the guy must be just like his father, so he was instantly on alert. In spite of being just a short, gangly kid, he jumped out of the truck to defend his grandfather.

Fortunately, there was no danger, just a down-on-their-luck couple with a broken fan belt, three hungry kids, and insufficient money for a tow truck. Gramps wandered to the back of the truck, grabbed his tool box and a flashlight and got to work.

"Don't just stand there, boy," he said. "Those young'uns are hungry. Get them something to eat." Jordan opened the cooler, which Gramps had loaded with smoked fish, jerky, berries, sunflower seeds, and apples. He took the cooler out of the truck and dragged it close to the car. The kids started squealing with happiness, and Jordan handed over every morsel to the hungry family.

Somehow Gramps worked his magic, and the car was road ready within the hour. Jordan placed the now empty cooler back into the truck as the family erupted into a

Empty Desk

chorus of thank-yous. Just before they took off, Gramps reached into his jeans pocket and pulled out a $20 bill, which he placed in the young father's hand. "Take care of those young'uns, now."

It was just a few more miles to the rest area where Jordan (then David) and his grandfather stopped for the night. Gramps turned off the radio and pulled a tattered camo jacket over his grandson. David thanked him, and Gramps reminded David to remember this special day, not just for the basketball game and meeting Michael Jordan, but for the family they had helped in their time of need. *Jordan learned that lesson well*, thought Nelly. *Exceptionally well.*

Before Jordan left, Nelly thanked him for sharing his story and commented that his grandfather would be exceptionally proud of the young man he had become. "You will have to bring in that jersey someday, Jordan. I would love to see it." "Oh, Ms. Nelson, I really, really wish I could show it to you. I don't have it anymore. It was one of the things that my father stole; he pawned it for drugs. Now that Gramps is gone, I wish I had it even more." He sighed, shrugged his shoulders a bit, wished her a good evening, then quietly left the room.

That's one remarkable kid, thought Nelly, as she too grabbed her bag and headed home.

Chapter 36

Nelly

The jumbled assortment of items that Nelly had removed from the secret drawer filled her with a satisfying blend of nostalgia, appreciation, and joy. Discovering Jenny Neberle's bright blue plastic band, though, immediately sapped her euphoria with a brutal reminder of just how short a life can be. Over the years, several of Nelly's students had lost their lives in unspeakable tragedies: car crashes, suicides, a mountain climbing mishap, and an accidental gunshot by a sibling had taken lives unexpectedly and far too soon. Each loss left a void in Nelly, but none so palpable as the death of Jenny Neberle.

Jenny was a wild child, full of a fierce but infectious enthusiasm for everything life had to offer. She entered or exited a room like a human tsunami, always whooping or hollering, a flurry of activity with every step. A mass of dark brown curls perched haphazardly all over her head, drooping playfully over her twinkling eyes, one a pale green, the other brown. Jenny was no scholar, but no one was more open to learning than she. She celebrated enthusiastically whenever she or any of her classmates did well, cursed a little when they did not, and otherwise just inspired others to keep on keeping on. She was only slightly concerned about her appearance and managed to avoid worrying about most things teenagers stressed out about.

Outside the classroom, she devoted what free time she had to a peer counseling group, where her acceptance of all differences made her a lifesaver in more ways than she even imagined. She was also a gifted basketball player, intimidating every opponent with her extravagant sweeps across the court, punctuated by whistles and shouts of encouragement to her teammates. She shouted out nonsensical phrases like *Toronto* or *Pony back, tiger front* to confuse and unnerve her opponents. On the court or in the classroom, she gave Nelly hope for the future whenever the tedium and stress of high school began to wear her down.

That promising future was put in question the last semester of Jenny's junior year. That year Jenny was just one of a pool of highly talented basketball players who went all the way to state finals. In that last game, Jenny went up for an easy layup before collapsing suddenly. She was carried off the floor and into a waiting ambulance, and her exodus from the game seemed to suck the energy from the room. Despite a commanding ten-point lead, her team stumbled, ultimately losing by a three-pointer at the buzzer.

Jenny returned to school the following week amid warm welcomes to which she responded with her usual high fives. She came by room 203 to pick up her homework from Nelly, and quietly revealed that her collapse had much more to do with her stage four ovarian cancer than a fall on the basketball court. The stunning news led to Nelly's firm resolve to do whatever she could to help this incredible young woman through what became fifteen rounds of chemotherapy and the last year of her life.

Jenny was somehow surprisingly ready for whatever challenge presented itself, but to the rest of her world-- family, friends, teachers, teammates, coaches, and classmates--stage four cancer signaled disaster. How could it be that a fun-loving, energetic, healthy and decent young woman with the whole world ahead of her had been infected with angry cells intent on destroying her very existence? How could the disease have progressed so rampantly without people knowing? Why had such a good person been singled out? How was any of this fair?

Jenny, warrior to the core, prepared herself for battle. She was determined to beat this and anyone who knew her better be on board. She demanded that everyone believe in her, in a successful journey to health, in miracles. She took stock of her resources, her friends, her faith, and her family.

She initiated her fight by hunting through every novelty store in a fifty-five-mile radius to find the perfect cancer-kicking symbol; she settled upon a Swiss alphorn, which had a particularly triumphant sound whenever she blew on it, which was often. She lugged the horn to every doctor appointment, lab test, and chemo treatment.

Before long, she took it to class as well, and teachers allowed her to use it to herald the start of every class and to summon any cancer-kickers or healing gods who might be lurking in the vicinity. The reassuring sound of the horn became a sort of auditory school mascot, incorporated into all the concerts and games and meetings that Jenny continued to attend in the waning months of her junior year.

While her friends and family members tried to hide their tears when her long beautiful dark hair fell out in clumps, she joked about how trendy she looked. She decided to personally design some "artsy" scarves to camouflage her bald head and thin limbs, sparking a contagious and widespread fashion trend throughout Horace Greeley

High School. As the school year wound down, she continued to lead the peer counseling group, to sing in the choir, and to pre-register for the toughest classes for her senior year. When she left for summer vacation with a breezy assurance in her best Arnold Schwarzenegger voice, "I'll be back," few doubted her.

Nelly was thrilled to see Jenny when she returned in the fall, but she arrived minus much more than her hair; the chemo had ravaged her body and the once beautiful eyes were slightly sunken and a pale shade of yellow. Within the first weeks of her senior year, she started to use a wheelchair to get around, ably assisted by a host of classmates who took it as a badge of honor to sound the horn to announce that Jenny was coming through. Throughout it all, her sense of humor and love of life remained fully intact, and whether it was in a stark hospital waiting room or within a crowded classroom or at the family dinner table--she managed to be, of all things, upbeat.

Many afternoons after school students would gather around her wheelchair as they sat and talked about the significant moments of their day; they grew to appreciate life a little more and came face-to-face with their own mortality. Sometimes, long after the last bell rang or the buses left, several students and teachers gathered around chattering about celebrations and competitions, music and art, collective plans and shared dreams. In this tightly knit group, a community bonded over the realization that this young woman epitomized everything they feared and everything they coveted about the human condition.

Through Jenny's example, many began to recognize what they had been missing: the first sip of a cold soda on a hot autumn afternoon, the cheers of young people as they crossed a finish line, the exquisite view of a bright blue sky. They named the trees on campus after their favorite heroes and encouraged their friends to quit being so mean. They became less concerned about a low grade or not having a date or whether it was too cold outside. They forgave their disgruntled parents and teachers, and often overlooked petty high school annoyances. They cared less about things and a lot more about people. They complained less and laughed more. At the center of this transformation sat Jenny cheering them on.

The days grew shorter and Jenny grew weaker. When she could no longer attend school regularly, her friends came to her home with homework assignments, gossip, and constant reassurances that she had a large army of folks who loved her. As her cancer cells multiplied, so did the many random acts of kindness from classmates and neighbors. No one asked what Jenny needed; they just knew.

Some filled her parents' gas tanks when they were not looking. Others raked the beautiful autumn leaves into huge piles and toasted smores over bonfires. They baked cinnamon rolls and lit sparklers in the evenings. The choir teacher and acapella group came to her neighborhood to perform an impromptu concert as she sat on her front porch. The yearbook photographer captured Jenny's last visits from her lifelong friends. The pep band even practiced on Jenny's street, parading through the neighborhood as dozens of little kids marched along behind them.

Then came homecoming. A half-dozen senior boys, each in a rented tuxedo and carrying a single red rose, arrived at Jenny's door to fetch her for the dance. By this time, she weighed just ninety pounds and could no longer walk.

As one of the guys blew her Swiss alphorn, the others lifted her tenderly out of her chair, raising her above their heads and placing her carefully in the limousine. Her brilliant smile, undiminished by disease and an uncertain future, flashed like a lighthouse beacon. She wore a gorgeous blue gown that had once been her grandmother's and had been expertly altered to fit her perfectly. On her right arm she sported six fragrant corsages from her multiple dates for the evening; on her left was her omni-present bright blue elastic band with the words *Cancer Can't* embossed on it.

Nelly had been one of the chaperones for that homecoming dance, and every single person who attended wore Jenny's bracelet. For a few special hours, her message prevailed. *Cancer can't: can't stop us, hurt us, or take away the evening.* The evening culminated with Jenny being crowned queen as six senior guys performed a perfectly choreographed medley of love songs. Then came dancing with wild abandon, boisterous shrieks of teenage laughter, and pleas for the night to never end.

Not long afterwards, Jenny stopped coming to school altogether. No more wheelchair races through the halls. No longer a Swiss horn announcing the start of class. The afternoon gatherings and discussions in the schoolyard stopped. When Jenny died on November 2, 2006, word spread quickly around Horace Greeley High School. Before nightfall, the lawn chairs, lit candles and fragrant flowers lined the street in front of the school, filled with subdued teenagers recounting memories.

Jenny had taught them more than any A.P. class or teacher. They had learned the lesson that what's tragic is not so much dying as it is not living the life one has. As they hugged, laughed, sang, and prayed long into the night, it was clear that the last earthly year for the vivacious 18-year-old cancer warrior, daughter, teammate, student, and friend had been, in fact, remarkable.

Nelly traced the letters on Jenny's blue bracelet but could not bring herself to pack it with the other items she had saved. She kissed it tenderly before slipping it into her pocket.

Chapter 37

Jordan

Jordan Michael's graduation day started with an uncharacteristically dark and overcast sky. Occasionally, a beautiful blue hue punctuated the skyscape, and Jordan thought how much the view was an apt metaphor for his high school experience.

Ms. Nelson would be proud that I saw my life in metaphorical terms, he mused, as he looked at his cap and gown and gold cord hanging on the bedroom door. *This is it*, he thought. *Now is my time, and with a degree and a little more luck, I will finally have my chance.*

He thought briefly of his father, wondering if he were still locked away in some prison and grateful that he would not be around to interfere in any of the day's activities. He sent up a silent message to Gramps, acknowledging that his sacrifices, some of them illegal, had enabled Jordan's getaway to Colorado and more importantly, this graduation day. Jordan promised Gramps that he would pay his sacrifices forward, then smiled as a vivid memory stream of fishing trips, berry picking, and fixing things flashed before him.

His reverie moved to his mother, and Jordan got emotional knowing that she would not be allowed to attend the graduation. After months of suspicion and worry, Jordan discovered Judith's horrible secret: she had become addicted to meth. As smart as Jordan was, he still had blinders on when it came to his mother. After all, she had been the one to successfully facilitate the whole identity switch and move from Ohio for the two of them.

Likewise, she managed to get him into school, secure a job, pay the bills, and cheer him on for the vast majority of his high school years.

A few months before graduation, though, he started to notice subtle changes in his mother. By this time, she had left her position at Walmart, informing her son that she could make more money cleaning houses instead. She had done that kind of work previously, so the ruse worked for quite a while. Often, she was awake early and left the apartment long before Jordan woke up for school. At first, she hid her problem well, and assured her son that her recent weight loss and inability to sleep was just stress.

Later Jordan spotted a crumpled aluminum can with a hole in its side in the trash, and something about it seemed strange. He shrugged it off, but the appearance of an ugly red sore marring Judith's normally flawless complexion coupled with dilated pupils alerted Jordan that there was something much more dangerous going on.

Jordan blamed himself for being so caught up in his senior year and the overtime hours at his job to understand the obvious signs of Judith's imminent descent into an increasingly dark place. He resolved to confront his mother and to help her, but first he had to finish his A.P. exams and complete his work assignment on the remodeling project of Gracious Manor's west wing. As soon as he could get these tasks off his plate, they would have a long talk.

One night, after finishing the second shift at his job, Jordan headed home intent on catching a few hours of well-deserved sleep. Even though it was well past 3 a.m.,

Empty Desk

the door to their apartment stood slightly ajar, a loud latenight infomercial spilling out into the hallway. Jordan burst into the room, and found his mother sprawled across the floor, convulsing and foaming at the mouth. A cell phone and packet of white powder had slipped from her hands, and the truth hit Jordan square in the face. He let out a pitiful cry, reached for his phone, dialed 9-1-1, then raced to help the now unconscious Judith.

Once the paramedics arrived, they were able to stabilize her before transporting her safely to North Colorado Medical Center. There a weary late-night team quickly assessed her condition, recognizing instantly the telltale signs of meth addiction. As she gradually came around, her only concern was for Jordan. He had not been allowed to accompany her in the ambulance, and she was both humiliated and worried sick that her actions might do something to damage his future. Meanwhile, Jordan had been unable to find the truck or the keys, so he started walking the several miles to the hospital; his frantic calls along the way produced no results. Hospital personnel were bound by strict confidentiality rules, and they were not about to say anything to an almost incoherent teenager.

Jordan ran as much of the way as possible, and after arriving to the emergency room, he gave the hospital workers as much information as he could, remembering their carefully rehearsed story of a previous life in Michigan. Neither one of them had a local doctor, a fact that the intake secretary found very strange, but it had been a long night, and there would be a shift change in a few minutes, so she processed the paperwork without too many questions. Jordan was then allowed to see his mother, who by this time had been transferred to a regular hospital room.

Their reunion was an emotional one. Judith begged Jordan to forgive her and promised that she would never take another drug. Jordan had heard other well-meaning assurances in his life and knew immediately that this would not be something she (or he) could handle without professional help. After learning that instead of cleaning houses she was really peddling drugs, he began to understand how this had all come about. He asked her if she would agree to go to rehab. She reminded him that without insurance this was impossible, but that she could and would do this on her own.

"We can sell the truck, use the money I saved for college, and I can quit school. You must do this, Mom. You have to." Judith was still in a fog, but the desperation on Jordan's face made her realize what she had almost cost him. "The truck is gone, Jordan. I'm sorry. And you cannot give up your college funds. There is no way in hell you can quit school. Not now. Not after all we have been through."

Dr. Sutton had quietly entered the room and witnessed this exchange. The situation resonated with him, not just because of his long tenure in the field, but also since his own sister had died of a heroin overdose. He had spent nearly a half century helping addicts come clean, but he also knew the dismal odds of successful recovery. However, Judith's test results and the earnest young man in the scene before him gave him hope that this case could lead to a successful outcome.

He cleared his throat to let the two know they were no longer alone in the room. "Excuse me for interrupting," he said. "Tonight is not the time to make these decisions, Mrs. Michaels. We have medication here to enable you to withdraw gradually. We will monitor you carefully, but the next few days will be the hardest ones of your life. After that, I can arrange rehab for you, and there is a way to do it without your son dropping out of school or the two of you going without transportation. For now, I want you to rest. Your body has gone through an incredible trauma, but I will be with you every step of the way."

Something about the disheveled physician with the long white hair and beard calmed both Judith and Jordan. He glanced at the teenager but directed his next comments to Judith, "As for your son, he needs to go home, and do whatever it takes to stay in school. His only job right now is to be a student. And you--you need to be the real adult." Judith nodded, releasing a thin stream of wet, sloppy tears and quiet sobs. The doctor turned to Jordan. "Young man, your mother is going to make it, trust me on this. The best way you can help her is to finish school and live the life you deserve. Now get out of here. Take my card. Call me whenever you need to, and I will update you. Within the next few days I will let you know all the details about your mother's recovery."

In the week that followed, the kind-hearted doctor kept Jordan at bay while his mother struggled through each stage of withdrawal. She went through periods of hallucinations, cravings, depression, and intense anxiety; as she fought for sobriety, Dr. Sutton assembled Judith's rehabilitation plan. Along the way, he kept in close contact with her son, who impressed Sutton with his maturity and selflessness.

Technically, Dr. Sutton should have referred Jordan to the Department of Social Services, but he when he learned of his spotless employment record and proximity to graduation, he circumvented their involvement. Too often the well-meaning but understaffed government agencies just complicated situations like this one.

By securing funds from a federal block grant, Judith was able to enter a comprehensive 90-day rehab program in Utah. The requirements were strict: absolutely no drugs or alcohol, intensive physical and mental health therapy, no visitation from family or friends, and limited phone contact. On Jordan's graduation day, she was 63 days in, and she had successfully met every single expectation and milestone. Jordan had gotten permission to speak to her at length the night before and assured her that he would carry her in his heart as he crossed that graduation line.

He had planned to either walk or take the bus to the graduation ceremony, but Ms. Nelson offered to transport him and to treat him to lunch afterwards. He had confided in his teacher about everything: how they lost their only vehicle, Judith's overdose, her drug dealing, her rehab, the fact that he was living alone. After all the secrets he had already revealed to her, he trusted her completely, and he was secretly relieved that he would not have to spend the entire day all alone.

He finished getting ready, checking his tie the way his old friend Mr. Stevens had shown him. He had polished his well-worn shoes the night before, ironed his shirt, and even sewn a button on his suit jacket. He had splurged on a haircut and some sweet-smelling hair gel. Even to the modest Jordan, the figure in the mirror looked darn impressive.

Before leaving, he reached into the desk drawer and retrieved the thick envelope that Mr. Stevens had given him several months previously. His instructions to Jordan had been to keep it sealed until after he received his high school diploma. Having something to open on this important day made it even more special, and Jordan planned to share its contents with Ms. Nelson. Since he had already imparted the story of Mr. Stevens to her, Jordan figured she would enjoy finding out the envelope's contents as much as he would. He slipped the envelope into his pocket before turning out the lights and locking the apartment door. With a slight skip to his step, he headed to the parking lot where Ms. Nelson had told him to meet her.

Ms. Nelson greeted her student with a huge smile. "Good morning, Jordan. You look great. Are you ready for today?" Jordan got into the car with a heartfelt thank you, and the two eased into a comfortable conversation about graduation, final exams, and Jordan's acceptance into the engineering school at the University of Colorado. They arrived at the stadium with time to spare and parked in the area reserved for faculty. Before heading their separate ways, they agreed to meet back in this spot after the ceremony.

Nelly always loved graduations, and this one was no exception. As the senior choir members assembled to sing a powerful version of the national anthem, the graduates walked onto the staging area in groups of four, then separated into pairs to make their way to their assigned seats. The bleachers were packed with cheering friends and families, united for a few hours in celebrating something wonderful. For some of these young people, making it to this moment was nothing short of miraculous.

Jordan was indeed one of these miracles, mused Nelly. She would miss their afternoon conversations, but she rejoiced that despite the obstacles, this young man would continue to change the world. She recalled his many secrets and the bizarre and dangerous circumstances that had brought him to Greeley. She thought about the multiple simple acts of kindness that he had performed so routinely, from fixing broken desks to building birdhouses for senior citizens. Then there were the life-changing moments that he brought to skillful and positive ends: the thwarted school bombing, the rescue of a young woman from the arms of a predator, the transformational invitation to a suicidal girl to a dance, not to mention his unconditional acceptance and love for his drug-addicted mother. She would be sad if this were the end of his story, but she knew in her heart that this was only the beginning.

The ceremony ensued with the customary fanfare, laughter, nostalgia, and speeches. Nelly greeted the parents of some of her favorites, chatted with her colleagues, and hugged several of the graduates as they came racing across the grounds with shrieks of "Nelly, Nelly, I am gonna miss you!!!!" After fulfilling her duty of handing out district brochures as the visitors left the stadium, Nelly returned to the parking area, where a smiling Jordan Michaels stood patiently waiting.

"Where would you like to have lunch?" Nelly asked. Jordan had never even considered calling Ms. Nelson *Nelly* like so many of his classmates did. He would forever hold her in high esteem, and the thought of telling her where to take him to eat would be just plain rude. "I have no preference. Whatever you choose will be perfect." Ms. Nelson thought briefly, then headed to Farmer's Inn, a small out-of-the-way Mexican restaurant with good food and service. Before entering the restaurant, she reached under the car seat to retrieve the graduation present she had bought for Jordan.

They spent the better part of the next two hours enjoying home-made burritos, spicy queso sauce, and cinnamon sopapillas as they reminisced about Jordan's journey. As the time came for them to leave, Ms. Nelson pulled out the gift she had so carefully wrapped for the occasion.

"You did not need to do this, Ms. Nelson," Jordan protested, "You have already done so much for me." "Just open it, Jordan. I hope you like it." Jordan deliberately took his time, savoring the solitary gift of the day. He read the card out loud: *To Jordan, whose story is still unfolding. May the days ahead be filled with peace, knowledge, and success. Thank you for including me in this chapter of your life. I will forever be your friend. Love, Ms. Nelson.*

Once he opened the box, he found a #23 Chicago Bulls jersey signed with Michael Jordan's unmistakable scrawl folded neatly inside. He sat for a moment in stunned silence as he reached out to touch Ms. Nelson's hand. "I can't believe it. Where did you find this? I can't believe you even remembered. Oh my God." One look at Jordan's face was all it took for Nelly to understand how much this act meant to Jordan. Never had such a time and money-intensive search for the perfect gift been so worth it.

The pair left the restaurant with full stomachs and hearts; theirs was a relationship that would stand the test of time. Ms. Nelson eased unto the highway, heading east to drop Jordan off at his apartment. He explained his plans to work double shifts to pay for college and to help his mother once she left rehab. He had earned a decent academic scholarship, but it fell short of paying for the many expenses of CU. Nelly assured him that his resourcefulness had no limits, and that today was not the day to worry so much.

Just before they reached the final exit, Jordan remembered the envelope in his pocket from Mr. Stevens. He reminded Ms. Nelson of the story of his much senior friend, and she urged him to open it. "He sounded like he regarded you highly. I bet it is something special. Go ahead, open it!" Jordan carefully unsealed the envelope, then scanned the first page of the thick document before nearly collapsing. His response was so visceral, so immediate, that Nelly could not tell at first whether he had received good news or bad news.

"What is it, Jordan? Tell me."

"If this is true, Ms. Nelson, I just inherited half a million dollars," Jordan stammered. "Half a million dollars."

Nelly had an emotional outburst of her own, a rather maniacal laugh that she could just not hold back. "That is awesome, Jordan, incredibly, miraculously awesome." *Finally,* she thought, *finally a decent thing happens to a decent person. No one deserves this more.*

Jordan and Nelly spent a little time scrutinizing the papers before they parted, and Nelly left convinced of their legitimacy. She promised to transport Jordan to the lawyer's office the following week, where the secretary for the firm of Mackey, Phillips, and Thomas officially confirmed that Jordan Michaels had no need to worry about paying for college or getting transportation any longer.

Chapter 38

Nelly

Several hours had passed since Nelly had started the slow but steady excavation of her secret drawer. Suddenly the urge to leave overcame her; she searched the drawer for the few remaining items, grabbed them without careful inspection, and filled the waiting duffel bag to the brim. *It has been a good run, but this is it. This is what remains of decades of life as a high school English teacher*, she thought. Scanning her classroom, once so alive with teenagers, now submerged in an eerie quiet, she felt content. It was as if the ghosts of those hundreds of students had paused, as she had, to take inventory of all the stories.

She gave the desk drawer one final shove. It snapped firmly into place like an alert soldier, giving off a jolting thud that echoed across the room. Perhaps some future teachers might discover it one day and be intrigued by why it was there; perhaps they might imagine stories about its former contents. Nelly hoped so. She mentally thanked Javier for creating it for her so many years ago.

Nelly, suddenly tired from the emotions of the day, reflected on how this had been the perfect finale. It had been better than too many pitchers of Coors with her exhausted colleagues. Better than one of those god-awful slide shows in which someone who did not even know her would try to summarize her decades of teaching. Better than some fawning new teacher trying to flatter her with some nonsense about filling her shoes.

This was the way she wanted it to end, with the powerful memories of equally powerful stories. She chuckled thinking of kids like Harley, Alex, and Josh, and hoped they were continuing to find laughter in their lives. To survivors like Fatima, Julian, and Maria, she sent up a prayer for their continued success. To the hundreds of others—like Darren, Mary, and Zach—she silently saluted them for teaching her so many lessons.

This was the last chapter of Nelly's teaching career, and although there was no way she could know it at the time, the beginning of yet another story. She stood tall, pleased about all that had transpired. She had made a real difference to students like Fatima, Tabitha, Dan, Harley, and many others. And they had returned the favor; she was convinced that at that very moment they were likely creating more powerful stories than she could even imagine.

She glanced at the now empty rocking chair, and for a moment she could see Jordan Michaels sitting in it as he had so many years ago, sipping a Coke and telling her his secrets. Nelly said a silent *thank you* to him and all the others, gathered up her belongings, glanced around the room for the last time, then shut the door, leaving the key in the lock before heading to the now empty parking lot.

Only a teacher can fully appreciate that first moment of freedom at the end of a long school year, that overpowering sense of fatigue followed by a shot of adrenaline. The knowledge that there would be no more papers to grade, lessons to plan, or meetings to attend filled her with an almost giddy euphoria.

Although she placed the duffel bag almost reverently into the passenger seat of her car, all the emotional nostalgia associated with it disappeared quickly, and she screamed out a celebratory *Whoop! Whoop!* as she got into her car.

Empty Desk

She buckled her seatbelt, turned the key in the ignition, backed up, and headed for the exit. In a final act of defiance to the school district, she deliberately ignored the newly painted direction arrows in the parking lot.

As she entered the street heading to the highway, she noticed how the trees swayed ever so gently in the wind, as if they were waving her home. Already some little kids were racing bikes and blowing bubbles as they screamed with delight. A lazy brown Lab ambled in a yard nearby, a neon-colored chew toy dangling from his mouth. All felt right with the world. Nelly located the oldies channel on the radio, cranked up the volume and belted out a few verses of John Denver's "Take Me Home, Country Roads" as she contemplated her upcoming summer plans.

The last verse of the song was playing as Mark Allen, drunk from far too many Happy Hour shots, misjudged the passing distance and slammed his black Chevy pickup into the driver's side of Nelly's Nissan with monster force. The collision upset the steady traffic flow, as travelers quickly pulled off the road to assist, or in some cases, just to gawk.

Mark emerged rather groggily from his truck, surveyed the damage he had caused, and unleased a string of profanity. The blood oozing from his forehead was barely perceptible as it dripped onto the faded Broncos jersey that had already absorbed a couple of beer spills from earlier that afternoon. Once he glanced at the twisted wreckage and the unconscious driver sandwiched in the car, Mark realized that his brief foray into married life and full-time employment was likely over. He staggered in an uncertain pattern, kicking shards of shattered glass as he pounded his fists on the hood of his truck.

Empty Desk

Nelly lay pinned in the mangled mess that had once been her car. The weight of the car door pressed tightly against her shoulders and hip, a thin rasping noise providing the only sign that she was even alive. As people tried frantically to free her and to restrain the now frantic Mark, shrill sirens announced the arrival of an ambulance and two police vehicles. The paramedics rapidly assessed the situation, issuing clear instructions to willing helpers, and miraculously and expertly excavated Nelly. As one of them treated Mark's minor injuries, a police officer prepared to take the obviously intoxicated truck driver into custody.

The medics placed a neck brace around Nelly and did their best to bring her around. Unable to revive her, they secured her carefully on the gurney and loaded her onto the waiting ambulance. A sinister-looking bystander spotted the stuffed duffel bag that had tumbled from the wreckage lying by the side of the road. He carefully picked it up, gathered a few spilled items, checked the attached identification tag, and carried it to his parked car. He tossed it in the back seat, started his engine, then drove away.

It would be three long weeks into Nelly's retirement from teaching before she would emerge from a coma. Unbeknown to her, she had already gone through two surgeries to repair damage to her shoulder and hip, multiple stitches to close deep gashes where her head had struck the windshield, and several brain scans to determine if she were suffering from a traumatic brain injury.

Somewhere from the deep foggy abyss of her unconscious state, she started to connect randomly with the outside world. At first, she saw brief flashes of light or heard the steady *ping, ping, ping* of some medical device. As hard as she tried to communicate, it was impossible; with each climb to the surface, she felt a sudden descent into quicksand so murky that she wondered if she were already dead. Gradually she deciphered the voices of people discussing her care, making dismal comments about nursing homes and vegetative states.

Nelly concentrated on surviving. Surely, she could not be dead or dying if she could still get upset over the lousy grammar of those who hovered around her. She winced in agony at a nurse's statement, "I done what could." *Patience*, she thought, *practice some patience.*

Nelly lost any sense of time, and she eventually had to put up an intense fight to even care. After an eternity of frustration, and just as she was about to surrender herself to the gloom, she heard a voice that was strangely familiar singing the lyrics of "Wind beneath My Wings" softly in her right ear. The tune was so enchanting, so heartfelt, so plaintive that just like that, she opened her eyes.

Immediately the singer with the golden voice let out a gasp followed by a rowdy cheer. "Nelly, Nelly, you're back!!!" She did not immediately recognize the man who stood before her, but as he continued to reassure her that she was "back," his distinctive voice triggered something from a distant past.

"How do you know my name? Where am I? How did I get here? What happened?" Nelly could not tell yet if she had spoken these words or if they were still buried in the recesses of her mind. She tried to sit up as she adjusted to her new normal, suddenly terrified of the unfamiliar surroundings and the strangers who hovered around her.

Empty Desk

The man with the golden singing voice shooed away the others in the room, pulled up a chair, and grasped her hands as he told her: "You have been in a serious accident, Nelly. You have been through two surgeries to repair a mightily damaged hip and shoulder. You checked out for quite a while; it has been several weeks since you have been with us. I am certain, though, that you are a survivor; it may take a little while, but you are going to make it."

Nelly stared at the man as he gradually came into clearer focus. How did she know him? Once the shadows faded, she glanced at the stethoscope first, then let her eyes travel across the curly brown hair and handlebar mustache before settling on the name tag. It read: Dr. Darren Autoby, North Colorado Medical Center. Darren!! The very same golden-toned tardy boy from her early years as a teacher. Here he was all grown up and a doctor—a real doctor.

She tried to communicate with him, to reveal how good it was to see him, to ask him about his journey through medical school. He raised his right hand to signal that she should calm down. Something about the familiar gesture was oddly reassuring to her.

"Stop trying to talk for now," Dr. Autoby said, "There will be plenty of time for us to get to know one another again. What is important now is that you give yourself a chance to rest. Let go of all that worry. I will be with you every step of the way." She believed those reassuring words and let herself slip back into a comfortable sleep.

When she awoke, she spotted Dr. Darren Autoby sprawled next her in the recliner where he had spent the entire night. He immediately came out of his slumber,

Empty Desk

smiled at his former teacher, and checked to see how she was feeling. After a few pokes and prods, he informed her that she was hereby officially on the mend.

He started to laugh softly in relief and asked her if she recalled him singing "You've Lost That Loving Feeling" in class so many years before. Before she could even reply, he sweetly serenaded her in a performance so touching that everyone in the hallways stopped to listen.

Although Nelly could feel the rather intense pain in her hip and shoulder, she knew that before long she would be able to start enjoying her retirement from teaching. In the additional days she spent in the hospital, she followed the therapist's instructions exactly and began to walk once more. Dr. Autoby stopped by often to sing to her. They reminisced and made plans to meet for coffee from time to time.

When the day came for Nelly to depart, Dr. Autoby stopped by for one more solo. He belted out a flawless rendition of "Stairway to Heaven" before dragging an overstuffed duffel bag into the room.

"The day you were admitted, a man dropped this off in the emergency room. We have been holding it for it a month now. I thought it might be important to you. The guy left his card with a note for you."

Nelly had not thought about the bag during her lengthy hospital stay, but as soon as she saw it, she was overcome with emotion. Getting reunited with her treasure trove was the perfect send-off, and she mentally thanked the stranger who had so thoughtfully retrieved it for her. There was no way she could have ever replaced or even explained what the contents of that bag meant to her.

She smiled brightly before turning the card over to read it. Her smile faded almost immediately when she saw a familiar name from her recent past and a cryptic message scrawled across it. Suddenly feeling a little unsteady, she reached for the tray table for support.

Dr. Autoby realized immediately that something was not right. "Whooooaaaaa, Nelly. What is it? Is something wrong?"

He translated the look on his teacher's face, settled into a chair, and requested, as he had done so often many years before, "Oh, Nelly, tell me a story. It's time for a story."

And what a story it was.

Made in the USA
Middletown, DE
20 September 2024